NIGHTMARE'S
DANCE

Dreambound
Book One

By
Dakota Brown

Nightmare's Dance
A Reverse Harem Tale

Dreambound, Book 1

All Rights Reserved
Copyright © 2022 by Dakota Brown
Cover Design © 2022 Open World Covers

Inkwolf Press
P.O. Box 473
Ault, Colorado
80610

ISBN: 979-8-9864144-0-9

www.inkwolfpress.com

PRODUCED IN THE UNITED STATES OF AMERICA

10 9 8 7 6 5 4 3 2 1

DEDICATION

For Super Jes
Thank you for teaching me to fly.

ACKNOWLEDGEMENTS

Ideas for novels come from all over the place. At least for me. I take something I read here, a chance conversation there, and jumble the ideas around in my brain until they stick. I decided I wanted to set my story in a realm I'd not yet played in: Dream. Then the fabulous Vera Valentine—read her books—happened to mention that I should write an aerialist as a main character. This came up because I've been taking aerial classes for about a year now. I am learning both silks and lyra. It's super fun. I highly recommend you give it a try if you ever get a chance. All those ideas stewed together in my subconscious while I worked on finishing The Pizza Shop Exorcist series. Once I was close to being able to work on this set of books, I had a lengthy brainstorming session with Shoshanah Holl—totally check out her artwork. After all of that, I had some pretty solid ideas of my world, who my characters were, and their struggles. The words flowed relatively easily for this novel, leading to my favorite kind of writing. The kind that's slightly less difficult than normal writing. LOL. Anyway, thank you for taking a chance on my newest creation, and I hope you enjoy it as much as I am loving writing it.

A huge thank you to my editors, Rachelle Hobbs and Aeryn Havens. Thank you SO much for all your insights. Make sure you read their books!

Thank you to my proofing team, Angie Addams and R. Knight (read their books, too), Amanda-Jane, Dorrace,

Paula, and Kristen. Any remaining mistakes after their eagle eyes are all my fault. Darned typos breed I'm telling you.

I want to shout out a special thank you for my patrons on Patreon: Melynda, Yashira, Jacqui, Kori, Shay, Caitlin, FandomDancer, Vivian, Margaret, Teri, and Rachel. Thank you for your extra support.

And last, but certainly the most important, thank you, Readers, for picking up my book and devouring it, then asking for more.

CHAPTER 1

Ember

My excitement warred with nerves as I stood in the dark backstage and rubbed rosin on my hands. The gritty powder dried my skin, made it stickier, and aided my grip. Which was good, because my hands were coated in sweat. This was far from my first performance, and it wouldn't be my last, but I never quite got over the pre-performance jitters, no matter how many times I took to the air in front of an audience.

"Ember," my partner Geraint said, his soft Irish lilt music to my ears as he came up behind me and put his hands on my arms. "You're going to be fantastic, Spark." He leaned over and kissed my neck. My skin goose-bumped at his soft touch, but my nerves settled at the familiar move.

I grinned up at him, appreciating the contact and admiring the way the skin crinkled around his stormy gray eyes when he smiled at me. "So are you, my knight."

He planted a kiss on my forehead before taking the rosin from me. We had two acts in this show, the second, and the last. The announcer for the cabaret dinner theater we performed at four nights a week was just finishing his introduction for the first act, a new friend of mine and very talented lyrist, Casey Stoll.

This was not a family friendly performance, and Casey practically made love to her aerial hoop as she flowed through her routine. She made the skill and strength necessary to hang in the air and move fluidly from one pose to another in the metal lyra look effortless. The lighting and her costume added to the illusion of her sensual performance.

I'd seen the act so many times by this point, but I was still in awe of her abilities as I watched from the dark backstage area. She was truly giving it her all tonight on our last performance of the contract.

Geraint and I would be up next for our combined adagio and aerial straps routine. Taking a deep, calming breath, I leaned back for a moment into Geraint's solid warmth. The faint musty odor of old sweat from the backstage area mingled with the familiar whiff of my knight's personal aroma. He reminded me of the woods at home after a summer storm. Geraint was shirtless to best show off his muscles and wore white pants that fit him perfectly. That I managed not to trace the V his muscles made on his stomach had more to do with not wanting to smear rosin on him than it did with my self-control.

I wore a matching white leotard with panels that mimicked my skin tone to make it look like I wore a two-piece bikini. They were all blinged out to make us sparkle under the stage lighting. I loved the bling, and I'd spent more of my life in leotards than I had in street clothing, so the revealing costume was comfortable. It looked fantastic under the lights. Geraint was also used to being on display.

We'd danced and flown together since we were children, and never once had he dropped me in a performance—a secret nightmare of mine. It had been years since he'd dropped me in practice. I knew he'd always be there to catch me, and my own abilities were without question. There was nothing to worry about.

Pushing away the butterflies in my stomach, I made sure I had rosin everywhere we needed extra grip.

The roar of the cheering crowd had me standing tall, though they applauded for my friend. Soon, their gasps of wonder and cries of enjoyment would be for me and my knight.

The announcer praised Casey and called out for Spark and her Knight, our stage names. Geraint kissed the top of my head and then we were up.

The lights dimmed, the first strains of our music sounded, and I scampered out onto the stage and struck a pose while Geraint took his spot just out of view. The light came up, shining on me and basically hiding the audience from my view behind the intensity.

Our story for this piece of choreography was a classic damsel in distress saved by her knight in shining armor. My moves showed my distress, and I poured as much emotion as I could into the act as I spun around and finally collapsed backward into a swoon.

But no! My savior caught me before I hit the ground. The audience gasped, not having seen Geraint creep out of the shadows until his arms wrapped around me, saving me from what would otherwise have been a hard fall to the stage. He had a nearly supernatural ability to remain unnoticed if he wished it, and we used it to our advantage on stage.

He lifted me, and the music paused dramatically while we stared at each other, me feigning shock, him not having to fake his adoration.

The next minutes were a sensual dance of two people getting to know each other, a dramatic upbeat to the music as we mimicked a first kiss, and then my knight lifted me into the air. I slipped my hands into the black straps suspended from the ceiling—cleverly hidden by the lighting and stage design until I took to the air.

3

I loved flying in the straps, in the silks, and even in harder apparatuses like the trapeze and the lyra. They might leave more bruises, but they all gave me flight, and I lived for time in the air.

Geraint spun me by my ankle as I supported myself by my arms, back arched as I half turned myself toward the ceiling, strap and arm going under my back to keep me in position. After holding the pose for a moment and reveling in the familiar bite of the strap on my skin and the pull of muscles in my shoulder, I flowed through the shapes while my knight spun me until I went up into an arch, his hands under my back. I freed one wrist from the straps and turned, releasing it into Geraint's hand. My second favorite thing besides flying was having him in the air with me.

With a few steps, he took my hand and spun us in a wide circle as we showed the connection the knight and his lady formed as the music supported the story we created with soothing, sensual tones.

My knight released my hand, separating us, and the music picked up speed a little frantically. *The lovers were separated! Would they ever find each other again?* Our movements along with the music told our story. But yes, the lady and her knight found each other. The music became triumphant as we repeated our sensual dance, this time in the air. We entwined our arms, or our legs, or both as we flowed together from position to position, spinning and showing the love of the knight and his lady and the bond they formed through our dance.

Finally, I released the strap completely, spine arched as Geraint kept me from the ground with only an arm under my back.

Our spin slowed, and he lowered us both until we gracefully touched down. He lifted me above his head by the waist. Then he lowered me, as we finished our piece with another suggestive floor dance, until finally, we

4

leaned away from each other, arms gripped together, counterbalancing, and sank to the ground. Once we laid flat on the stage the lights went down and the audience cheered.

As soon as it was dark, we got to our feet and hurried off stage so the next act could go on.

"Damn, you two are fire together." Casey pulled me in for a hug, stopping me on our way to our dressing room. We had to change and make sure we touched up our makeup in time for the last act. It was our doubles silks routine.

"Casey, when are you going to marry that lyra?" I joked.

She laughed as she headed back to the stage to wait for her next piece, spinning LED poi. She said she preferred fire, but the venue couldn't handle the requirements for actual flames, so LEDs it was. "Ferdie and I are going for a long engagement." Ferdie was the name she'd given to her hoop.

We continued on our way.

"Geraint, that was perfect, as always," I said once we were in our dressing room. A glorified closet where we could store our things and change our costumes. The smell of our sweat mingled pleasantly from the aroma of fine dining drifting in from the restaurant. I loved the way our scents mingled and complemented each other, as if accenting how we belonged together.

If we hadn't had one last act, I would have pressed my lips to his and smeared our makeup all over our faces. Soon... Very soon I'd have my way with him in our apartment and then we'd be heading to one last private show our manager and rigger, Robby, had set up for us. After that, we had a summer at home teaching at my parents' fitness camp for kids and teens.

"You are a shining gem, my dear spark," Geraint replied, hugging me closely, though avoiding my hair and makeup. He winked. "Change for me."

Our last act was more of a BDSM display in the silks, our costumes black and our silks red. My leotard gave the illusion of straps all over my body. Geraint's outfit was all black with some flesh-colored panels and gave the illusion that he wore a collar at his neck while still protecting him from potential silk burns.

Happy to show off for my knight, I shifted my stance, swaying slightly to the music that filtered in from the performers now on stage. Sliding my hands up my body, I brushed them playfully over my small breasts, before hooking my fingers in the top and sliding it off one shoulder.

The heat in Geraint's eyes spurred me on, dampening my pussy and making me eager for the night to be over. I loved performing, but Geraint's attention to my body was another favorite thing of mine.

He darted his tongue out, licking his lips as I carefully slid the leotard off. The music accompanied my slow, sensual movements perfectly and, for a moment, I let the rhythm of the song take me away from the present. Fabric whispered against my skin as I folded in half then continued to push the costume down my legs, butt now up in the air and on display.

"You are lovely, my spark," Geraint rumbled.

I straightened in time to see him stalk toward me, a hungry, almost feral look in his stormy gray eyes that I absolutely loved anytime I could provoke it. My knight was usually so controlled.

We needed to keep moving and warmed up for our next act. *A quicky was movement, right?*

He seemed to be on the same wavelength, a smile playing at his lips, hands dropping to his waist to push his own costume off. I was well familiar with the pleasure that bulge in his pants could bring me. The anticipation of him freeing himself from his costume so he could cage himself inside me had me instantly wet.

A sharp rap on our door startled both of us.

"Twenty minutes, you two," Robby ordered. "Get dressed and get out here."

Geraint licked his lips again, and I could see thoughts of disobedience flickering in his eyes. I grinned and thrust my chest out enticingly.

"Now!"

"Damn it," my knight muttered, accent thickening with his displeasure.

"We're almost dressed," I called, unable to keep a sharp note of annoyance out of my voice.

"Sure you are," Robby replied. The likelihood that he realized what he was interrupting was very high. He knew us all too well.

"Probably for the best," I muttered so he wouldn't hear.

Geraint's hungry grin turned playful. "Probably," he agreed with me. "We'll just have to pick up where we left off tonight."

"Promise?"

"Anything for you, my spark," he replied.

I grinned and, after a moment to admire his muscular frame, I set about getting ready for our next performance. A quick drink, a half an energy bar, and my next costume. Geraint did the same, though he ate all his energy bar. I'd dive into the food later, but between acts I tried to keep it light. Just enough to keep my energy up.

Robby had confiscated my chocolate-covered expresso beans, saying if I needed to snack, I should snack on something better for myself. He was probably right, otherwise I'd live on the things. Next contract, I'd come up with a secret stash.

We touched up each other's makeup, studied our costumes to make sure everything was in place, and headed back out into the hallway to get our rosin and pointedly ignore Robby. He followed us, a smug grin on his face. The man was worth his weight in gold, but sometimes I wanted to strangle him. Like right now, when a quickie would have been just the thing to keep me going through our silks performance.

Casey hurried past us, poi dangling from her hands and a radiant smile on her face. "See you two at the after-party?"

"Yeah, Casey, wouldn't miss it," I said. It was the end of the show season for us. As much as I wanted to get laid, I had been working with these people for the last six months and I wanted a chance to say goodbye. In most cases, I'd work with them again soon, but some I might not see for years outside of social media, and it was important to say a proper farewell for now. Besides, I was never one to skip a party if I didn't have to.

We both did a little stretching, keeping our muscles warm while we waited for our turn.

When the announcer called for me and Geraint, we grinned at each other and headed out for our last act of the season with the cabaret.

***

I had a nice, comfortable buzz going when Casey, and Phillip, one of the contortionists, stood up and raised their glasses.

"Here's to a fantastic season together. I know some of you are staying on, and some of us are moving to new gigs. I just wanted to say I love each and every one of you, and I hope to work with you all again soon." Casey laughed. "I can't always say that at the end of a contract, but I truly mean it. You are all fantastic."

We raised our glasses.

Phillip singled out a few of the newer circus artists, praising how far they'd come in the last six months. We were all happy to drink to that. Then we broke off from the main table to mingle. I headed for the bar to get another drink and Geraint headed off to chat with some of the other performers.

I loved the show season, but I was looking forward to getting home. We had a comfortable routine for our summer months, and I needed the downtime.

"Are you and your Irish knight ever going to make it official?" Casey came up behind me.

"What?" I accepted my fruity drink and turned to face my friend. She took a minute to grab her own drink before gesturing for me to follow her to one of the standing tables where finger food waited.

"You and Knight?"

"Oh. You mean like get married or something?"

"It's so obvious you're totally into each other." She sipped her drink, a grin on her lips and eyes shining above the rim of her glass.

"I don't know. I mean, what we have works. Why mess up a good thing?"

I didn't tell her there was something holding him back. I had no idea what, but it had been hard enough to talk him into my bed in the first place, and I wasn't willing to push any further. I'd known Geraint most of our lives, but there were certainly things I didn't know, and he didn't like to talk about his past, so I'd never pushed.

"Besides, marriage isn't everything. We have a solid, committed relationship and a solid business partnership."

9

"As long as you're happy, Ember. That's the important thing."

I smiled and nodded. "I am."

"Besides, I'm one to talk. I've got a better relationship with Ferdie than I ever manage with anyone else." Casey chuckled and downed her drink.

"There's someone out there with the willingness to share your love with a metal hoop." I nudged her playfully.

"Oh, I know. I've even found a few. It just never seems to last. Okay, on to other topics or I'll get more drunk than I want to. You got a contract lined up for the fall yet?"

"I don't think so. Robby doesn't usually commit to anything until later in the summer. We've got one last gig, a private event tomorrow, and then we're heading home for Mom and Dad's summer camp like we always do."

"I envy you," she said. "You know that, right?"

"We could always use another teacher. May not pay what a contract does, but it's rewarding and comes with housing."

Casey smiled. "I'll think about it. Regardless, the reason I brought it up, I've got a line on a few potential gigs in the Caribbean for the winter."

My eyes widened at that. Spending the winter some place warm was always the dream. "That sounds amazing. I'll have Robby get in touch with you." White sand beaches, sun, and warmth all winter long. A lot of outdoor performances with those gigs. I loved it.

"Great. I can't wait to work with you again. Maybe we can develop that threesome act we talked about a few months ago." She mock leered at me.

Chuckling in response, I tilted my glass to her in a salute. "I'll totally think about it. If we do all end up on the gig, I bet we can work something out."

"Great!"

My knight caught my attention, a mischievous glint in his eye.

"I don't even have to look to know you're staring at your man. You're practically drooling."

"I mean, you've seen him shirtless, right?"

"Babe, I'm not saying you're wrong. I just know he's the one you're looking at, and I'm sure you're ready to get out of here and keep each other up for the rest of the night. Go on. Have Robby get in touch with me, and I'll see you this fall."

I refocused on Casey. "I'm serious. If something doesn't come up for the summer, we need another instructor. It's not a camp counselor type position, it's purely instruction. Gymnastics, aerial, things like that."

"What happens at this camp? You've mentioned it, but I've never thought too hard about it."

"All things gymnastics, plus a ton of outdoors activities. Some kids do day camp stuff, some stay for a week or two at a time. We have a handful who stay all summer while their parents travel. We have a great location. Just close enough to a big town for supplies and any potential medical needs, and far enough out that they have the wilderness to explore."

"Sounds amazing." She got a wistful look in her eyes that made me want to hug her.

"It was a great place to grow up. I love going back during the summer. Winters in Pennsylvania are colder than I prefer, so I don't usually stay and teach through the winter months."

"It must be something to have supportive parents."

Casey's folks thought her obsession with circus arts was immature and doomed to failure, despite her years of success as a performer.

"I guess it helps that Mom was an Olympic gymnast, and she met Dad through the sport. Their training camp has been successful because of their passion, and it has helped so many people."

"Tell you what, if I don't find something I like for the summer in the next few weeks, I'll call you and see if that position is still open."

"Deal." My eyes drifted back to Geraint. He'd gotten caught up in a conversation, but seemed to sense my attention and glanced back at me.

"Great, now go celebrate with that smoking hot man-candy of yours and I'll talk with you soon."

I hugged Casey and headed over to my partner, adding a bit of a sway to my hips that got his attention right away. His tongue darted out to lick his lower lip and the guy he was talking to turned and his gaze fell on me as well.

Though most of my attention was on my knight, I noticed that I'd affected the other man, too. His name was Pat, and he was one of the other contortionists. I'd always thought he was gay, but maybe he was bi?

Geraint said something to Pat, and they gave each other a quick hug. Then my knight strode toward me, grabbing me by my waist and throwing me over his shoulder before I could even yelp.

I kicked my feet in mock dismay until he pinned them against his chest and headed for the door.

"I assume you're ready to leave?" he asked once we were out in the hallway of the small restaurant where we'd booked a room for our party.

"Yeah."

"Good. Robby said he would see us tomorrow for brunch and not to worry about our gear." My partner's musical voice rumbled through me, and I sighed in satisfaction, staring at his ass while he carried me. "We've got a ride coming. Be here in two minutes."

"Thanks, Geraint. You always take such good care of me."

"Of course, I do." He shifted my weight over his shoulder, warning me that he was going to bring me to the ground. I let myself slide down his chest, arms hooked behind his neck, staying pressed against him, and planting my lips against his.

We kissed until his phone buzzed, warning us our rideshare was here.

The trip back to the apartment the three of us had rented for the contract was short, and I was practically vibrating with need by the time Geraint unlocked our door. I grabbed him and pulled him inside, only waiting long enough for him to get it locked behind us before I tugged at his tight-fitting t-shirt.

He let me pull it off him and toss it to the floor. My shirt quickly followed. We kicked off shoes and shed our clothing, leaving a clear path toward the bedroom we shared. If Robby made it home tonight, he'd grumble at us tomorrow, but it wasn't the first time we'd left a clothing trail through wherever we were living.

Our things were mostly packed, since we were leaving tomorrow, but we still had the necessities out, including our toys.

We were both naked by the time Geraint picked me up by the waist and tossed me onto the bed. I bounced lightly on my butt, striking a pose, knees spread wide, back arched, teasing him with the view.

My knight stalked forward, staring at my bare pussy, tongue flicking across his lips.

I couldn't wait to taste myself on his lips, and he knew it.

Growling, he grabbed me by the hips and dragged me down the bed until he could kneel in front of me. I put my legs over his shoulders, and he dove in, tongue caressing me, knowing my favorite spots from many years of practice.

Mewling, and thrusting against my partner's face, I rode the build of pleasure as he expertly worked me, sliding a couple of fingers inside and flicking them until the pressure crested and spread through me.

"Mmm, good start," I said in an endorphin and alcohol induced haze.

"Plenty more where that came from," he replied, standing and covering me with his body.

I tugged on his shoulder, pulling him down so I could taste the evidence of my pleasure on his lips. He obliged, pressing his mouth to mine, opening for me, the dance of our tongues as practiced as the dance we had performed in the air a few hours ago.

Once he was sure I was ready, he pressed against my entrance and, at my nod, worked his way inside.

Moaning at the delicious stretch, I angled myself to take him as deeply as I could in that position. Geraint got his feet under him then stood, grasping my hips with his hands, lifting my butt, and thrust into me, a satisfied groan escaping his lips as he caged himself inside me. We maintained that position for a solid build toward more orgasms before Geraint lowered my hips, kneeled on the bed, and pushed one of my legs to my chest, splitting my thighs and taking advantage of my flexibility. Then he really pounded into me. I panted, crying out as my orgasm built.

We crested together, limbs trembling, breath coming fast, as we shuddered in the aftershocks of our orgasms. We were quick for our first round, but we had a few hours left before we'd need to snatch some sleep prior to brunch, and Geraint wouldn't let the time go to waste.

CHAPTER 2

Ember

"Y ou two ready for tonight?" Robby, though he hadn't come back to the apartment until morning, was bright eyed at lunchtime, as always.

Geraint seemed unaffected by our late night, but I clutched my coffee like the lifeline it was.

"Yeah," I said. "I will be, anyway. Some exercise and a nap and I'll be good to go by this evening."

He grinned at me, delighting in my apparent misery. I had no regrets, except that I wasn't still in bed. Breakfast was tasty, however, so that helped some. Well, it was basically lunchtime, but I was eating breakfast foods.

"Why don't you two enjoy the rest of the afternoon? I'll finish packing and deal with the rental agency. We'll be on the road back to Pennsylvania before you know it."

Our manager knew I was eager to be home. We'd met Robby in high school, and he'd become fast friends with Geraint. It had taken a little while for him to grow on me, but by the time we were off touring, his knack for making connections and organization had proven itself repeatedly, and making him our manager had been a simple decision.

"Be careful with Max!" I ordered.

"Your precious succulent will be safe with me, Ember," Robby chided.

"It had better be." I aimed a fake frown at him before diving into the last of my breakfast.

Geraint laughed, though didn't object. He might have thought my concern for my little plant was silly, but he never actually said it. I'd "rescued" the poor thing from severe over watering. Soon, I'd be home amongst the gardens I tended through the summer, surrounded by my favorite flowers in my favorite landscape, rolling hills and old-growth forests. I itched to get some time where I didn't have to perform constantly, and I could relax and water flowers and draw my favorite landscapes. I had a couple of summer commissions waiting for me.

"Let's go to the park," Geraint suggested. "We can get some exercise in, and then you can take time to draw that pond you've been admiring all winter."

He always knew just what I wanted.

The weather was perfect, and I agreed immediately.

Geraint left me with Robby to go retrieve my sketchbook, and I sat in comfortable silence with my friend for a few minutes before I remembered my conversation with Casey last night.

"Oh, by the way, Casey has a lead on some Caribbean gigs for the winter. You should talk to her."

He perked up at that idea. "Excellent. I've had a few inquiries about our shows, but I'm still collecting information. We have a lot of interest, so I doubt we'll have trouble finding something to our liking."

I smiled at that. It hadn't always been that way. Before we had made a name for ourselves, the three of us took whatever gigs we could get. These days, people mostly came to us, but it had taken years to get to that point. Geraint and I had another solid decade of performing ahead of us, before we had to decide what was next. My parents wanted me to take over their school. Trouble was, they also wanted to at least partially retire sooner than I wanted to stop traveling. It was an increasingly uncomfortable conversation that we had more and more often. Mostly, I tried to avoid the subject. Mostly, they let me. Thirty was right around the corner, but I didn't figure I had to think about settling down until I was forty, at least.

I'd finished another coffee by the time Geraint returned with my sketchbook. We both gave Robby a quick hug before heading out to the park, hand in hand. My knight had my bag over my shoulder, and I trusted him to lead the way while I took in the sights.

After six months, this part of New York was very familiar to me. We'd had contracts in New York before, even in the city, but this was the first time I'd been in this area of the state. I enjoyed it, but I was peopled out. Of course, by the end of the summer, I'd be itching to get back on the road. Especially if we got a good gig where white sand beaches and crystal clear water were part of the deal.

"Casey wants to work on that act she's mentioned a few times if we get in the same gig together," I said after a few minutes of quiet.

"If you want to do it, you know I'm game." He squeezed my hand while we walked, his arm brushing against mine.

Geraint rarely objected to anything. He was so easy to get along with. About the only time we'd ever truly argued was when I'd been trying to find someone to hook up with, after he'd turned me down one too many times. For a while, I thought he'd finally agreed to join me in bed just to keep me from going after someone else. Still, we'd been together for several years now, and I never figured out what his objection had been. It was easier to let it go and just enjoy what he gave me. Like it was easier not to press on why he didn't want to get married. It truly didn't matter. He'd just never given me an answer that really made sense the handful of times I'd brought it up.

17

My knight found me the perfect vantage point to observe the lake while we sat in the lush grass and stretched out muscles that were stiff from use yesterday. I paid particular attention to my forearms and shoulders, though all of me got warmed up. Once I was ready, we jogged around the lake a few times before returning to the spot we'd stretched at. We didn't need a lot of exercise today, just enough to limber up. The entire process took about an hour.

Geraint caught more than one extended stare from some of the women enjoying the park and a few of the men. My knight was tall, muscular, and strong as hell. He had to be to haul me around in the air as effortlessly as he did. I was taller for a gymnast, and though I was lean and strong, I was not nearly as light as the smaller women in my field. Still, my knight and I had trained together since we were little, and he'd adapted as I'd grown.

We would repeat the stretching and warmup later before we performed tonight. After settling with my back against a tree, I pulled out my sketchpad and put my pen to the page.

At one point I noticed Geraint talking to someone, but he often did that as he wandered while I drew. I didn't think much of it, far more entranced with capturing the play of light across the water with my pen strokes than I was with who my partner talked to.

I lost myself in my work until the light angle changed enough to make me wonder what time it was.

Geraint settled next to me when I looked up. I angled my sketchbook so he could more easily see.

"Beautiful," he whispered, breath tickling my ear as he leaned in. "I don't recall demonic dogs down by the lake, however."

"What?" I looked more closely at my drawing. Sure enough, I'd added some heavily jowled dogs to the reeds by the lake. They looked out of the painting as if staring at me.

"Wow, I haven't done that in years," I said. Ash, my cousin, had always been giving me a hard time about my random fanciful additions to my landscapes. I never actually remembered drawing the creatures, they just showed up as if I hadn't been aware of their presence consciously, but my brain had acknowledged them by putting them down on paper.

My knight chuckled, though it sounded a little forced—unusual for him.

"What's up?"

"It's time for us to get dinner and prepare to head for the gig."

I wasn't sure if he was evading my question, or if I imagined that something seemed to be bothering Geraint. He was never bothered, so it must have been my imagination. I let it go, accepting his hand up after packing away my tools.

"You ready to get home?" I asked my lover.

"Yes, as ready as you are." Geraint squeezed my hand before releasing it.

I turned toward him, and he placed his hands on my waist. His short, sandy blond hair was silky against my fingers as I mussed it. "One more gig, a long overnight drive Robby swears he's fine with doing, and we'll be home tomorrow."

For once Geraint's smile didn't make it to his eyes. Something was bothering him, but before I could ask, he kissed me. This wasn't an everyday kiss, the kind I was used to receiving on the regular. No, this was a soul consuming, I-want-to-meld-with-you-and-never-let-you-go sort of kiss. I dug my fingers into Geraint's back and pressed my entire body to his. He clutched me against him almost painfully tight.

"I love you, Spark. I almost never say that, but I do. You know that, right?"

"I do, Geraint. What's wrong?" I frowned, worry chasing away some of the happy feelings that had spread through me moments before.

"I just wanted to make sure you knew." He kissed the top of my head and gave me a far gentler squeeze before releasing me. My knight picked up my bag and slung it over his shoulder, taking my hand and leading me back toward the road and presumably wherever we were eating for dinner.

He hadn't answered my question, and that nagged at me a bit. I would have to bring it up again later, but for now, we had a performance to focus on.

***

The lights went down, and I stalked out onto the stage, the red catsuit I wore shimmering in the stage lights. Geraint waited for me on his knees. That was always a lovely sight, especially when shirtless and displaying his impressive muscles, collared, and wearing tight-fitting black pants.

I didn't have to fake the desire on my face as I sauntered across the floor, my prop strap sliding through my hands. The music had a predatory tone I appreciated.

This was an adult party, and Geraint was risking some silks burns by being shirtless, but it was the last performance for a while, and he had decided to deal. His collar was fabric and a breakaway for safety in the air.

His eyes briefly lifted to meet mine, and I pointed at the floor. He dropped his gaze in submission. I reached Geraint's side, and the music turned playful.

I ran the strap over his shoulders. He shivered, and I put a finger under his chin and drew his gaze up to mine, before dancing around him, caressing him with the strap and claiming him with my moves.

My knight kept his eyes on me, posture remaining submissive. Once I drew him to his feet, he matched my steps, always letting me lead. The music turned sensual as we moved around each other.

At an uptick in the song, I swept my hand along his neck, then out as if I grabbed a leash. He followed, and I pranced over to the silks and gestured for him to climb. After I mimicked removing the invisible leash, he took to the air, powerful muscles flexing as he made his way up the silks. Not going to lie, I might have drooled on myself a little.

Geraint danced in the silks for a few moves, locking in a foot and posing, wrapping himself up and further adding to the bondage theme of our performance.

The crowd gasped when Geraint dropped, spiraling downward, the silks stopping him short of crashing into the ground. He worked his way upright and climbed back up the silks, this time hooking his legs into the loop we'd tied at the top. This was my cue to start up the fancy drapes— as a friend called them.

My climb was sensual, and when I reached the top, Geraint offered me his hands. We locked wrists, and I flew in his grip, twisting into provocative shapes and sensually wrapping myself around his body, climbing him, dropping into his arms, and dancing through our moves. Finally, he cradled my back, and I arched, feet and hands dangling toward the ground, stomach lifted toward the ceiling, the only thing between me and plummeting to the floor were his hands, but Geraint would never let me fall and I hung there while the crowd cheered. I'd almost forgotten about them for a moment, caught up in the silent communication with my knight in a dance we'd done hundreds of times.

As the music came to the transition, I reached up and shifted my weight until Geraint could maneuver so that we could clasp hands. Then I tangled my legs in the silks and transferred from his sure grasp to the grip of the silks. I twisted my legs until I hung by my hip and wrapped the fabric around me, setting up for a dramatic drop.

The music paused, and I let go as it crashed into a new segment. The crowd gasped again as I fell, then cheered when I came to a stop at the bottom, several feet above the floor. I flipped, holding my arms out and slowly descending the rest of the way to the ground before turning and pointing at Geraint, then toward the ground.

He reached for the silks and danced his way down, ending on the ground on his knees at my feet.

The audience cheered as the music ended.

I held out my hand to my knight and raised him to his feet before we both bowed and left the stage.

The show had other acts to entertain people and after a break, we were supposed to help serve drinks and stuff. Basically, fancy props. I didn't mind. The gig paid well, and we'd be out of here in another couple of hours and on our way home.

"Brilliantly flown, my spark," Geraint whispered in my ear as he wrapped his arms around me backstage.

"You as well, my knight." I grinned up at him. "Let's get changed and finish the night."

He nodded. Robby would be busy closing up the stage and taking down our gear so we could get out of here on time.

We hurried into the spare bedroom we were using as a changing area and switched into costumes more suited to handing out drinks. My knight was still shirtless, but I'd changed into a slinky dress covered in bling.

A quick kiss, some water, and a snack, followed by another slightly lengthier kiss, and we headed back out to circulate amongst the people.

***

Though being a fancy serving girl was my least favorite type of gig, I'd enjoyed the actual performance earlier. Geraint balanced on a trapeze we'd rigged for the purpose, and people came to him for champagne. It kept him a little farther away from the random grabby hands of inebriated partiers. He didn't mind a little random petting, but sometimes it got excessive. This group was remarkably well behaved, though the kink community tended to be respectful, even drunk.

I stayed close to the bar in case I needed to help Geraint out, but he was currently laughing with a couple of ladies and didn't look like he needed saving. The bartender changed out my spent bottle of red for a fresh one, and I moved back into the crowd.

"Your performance was so amazing," a woman dressed in a black catsuit said as I topped off her glass.

"Thank you." I smiled graciously, genuinely appreciating the compliment, but even after all these years, not sure what to say when given one.

"Yes, quite remarkable. You must have been practicing for years to get this good," a man said, coming up behind me.

I twisted around and held my hand out for his empty glass.

After a quick hesitation, he handed it over, and I filled it before answering. "Yes, since I was a child. My parents were gymnasts and my mother also got into aerial. She has a school." Probably more information than the guy needed, but something about the calculating expression in his eyes freaked me out, and I over explained to hide my reaction.

After a brief hesitation, he smiled, but it didn't reach his eyes. I shivered and looked away. There was nothing overtly threatening about him. He was just your average white guy, average brown hair with a nondescript cut, though his eyes were a smoky gray that reminded me a little of Geraint's. Maybe it was the way he moved? He seemed to flow through his motions a little unnaturally.

"Tell me, do you like hiking, or...?" He hesitated again, as if looking for a word. The man didn't have an accent that I could detect, so if English wasn't his primary language, I couldn't tell. "Playing, I suppose, in the outdoors."

What a weird-ass question for the circumstances. "Yeah, I suppose." I didn't want to tell him how much I like the outdoors. Suddenly, I didn't want to tell him anything at all.

I turned away, glancing for my knight. He'd slipped down off the trapeze and was already heading my way.

Geraint reached my side, though he didn't put his arm around me as I'd hoped.

"Knight," the creepy man said, making it sound more like a title than Geraint's stage name, or last name.

Geraint's jaw clenched and his skin paled before he took a deep breath and inclined his head politely. "Can we help you with something?" He offered the bottle of champagne he held.

"Ahh, your partner already filled my glass."

A few of the women Geraint had been talking to earlier came over, giggling drunkenly. Two draped themselves on my knight, and one put her arm over my shoulders. They all tugged us away from Mr. Creep, laughing the entire time.

That Geraint let it happen, made me believe they were purposefully saving us, not being excessively handsy. Fortunately, the creep left the room. As soon as he was gone, the women released us, sobering a fair bit. "Looked like you two needed saving," one of the women, a cute-as-a-button blond, said. Her cornflower blue eyes were kind, and I wanted to hug her and cry, though I had no idea what provoked that amount of emotion. I really felt like we'd been saved from something terrible.

"Do you know him?" I couldn't help shuddering.

"No. He's not a regular. No idea how he got an invite, or slipped past the bouncers. We're an exclusive group." Wrinkles marred her pale brow as she stared where the creep had retreated to. "Oh, well. He's gone now. You two are fabulous." Her exuberant grin returned, and the other two women showered us with praise.

Blushing, I glanced at the floor.

This time, Geraint's hand found my shoulder and squeezed. "My spark is amazing."

I just about melted at the adoration in his voice. "You're amazing," I shot back, not quite able to take the full brunt of the praise.

"Have you two known each other long?" The woman with the cornflower blue eyes looked between us.

The creep must have put me on edge because the innocent question had me tensing up again. We got asked that question constantly, and it had never bothered me before.

"A year or two," Geraint replied with a smirk.

That was not his normal answer. Maybe I was right to be on edge. We usually told people we'd grown up together.

I kept my stage smile plastered on my face. *What was going on?*

"I believe we've reached a much-needed break," Geraint said gently. "Mind if I steal my spark away?"

"No, thank you for the magnificent show." She included both of us in her praise.

Geraint favored her with his best smile. The one that melted panties off women. I could almost see the three ladies get wet under his full attention. Normally it would have had me anticipating more once we were alone, or dragging him off to a private room, but not tonight. Right now, something was wrong. I didn't like it one bit, so I kept the stage smile plastered to my face and let Geraint lead me first to the bar where we dropped off our bottles, then out of the dining area to the back room.

"I think that's enough for tonight," Geraint said quietly after he shut the door. "Let's go. If they're cranky, we can refund some of the money."

"Yeah, tell them I got a headache or something." I shivered. "Geraint, why was that weird? Nothing about that should have been weird."

My knight sighed and shook his head. "I don't know, Spark. Let's get changed and get home."

Happy to take the simple route, I quickly slid out of my dress and into some yoga pants and a long, colorful jersey top that covered my butt. Geraint stuffed our clothing into our bags—the dress needed dry cleaning anyway—and shouldered them.

The soft party music filtered through the closed door, and I could make out the mixed smells from the kitchen over the faint whiff of sweat both Geraint and I exuded. A shower would have felt amazing, but I wanted to get out of there more than I wanted to make use of the attached bathroom. The unease lodged in my throat and made it hard to breathe.

Geraint came over and put his arm around me. "We'll be okay, Spark. Come on, let's get out of here."

I leaned into his familiar embrace for a few moments, believing him. He always took care of me.

That he hesitated by the door, listening before he turned the brass knob and looked out into the hallway before gesturing for me to follow, freaked me out.

Throat tight, heart racing in my chest, I followed. Why was I so afraid? There was no reason that either of us should be on edge. Still, I didn't object when Geraint pushed us back into a bathroom and shut the door, moments before someone came striding down the hallway. Adrenalin surged with every determined, heavy thump of the person's shoes on the wooden floor. I assumed it was a man from the weight behind those steps, but it could have been a larger woman, too.

Geraint nearly held his breath, and my exhalations sounded harsh in my ears. Surely whoever it was could hear my heart pounding in my chest? The rasp of my breath? I tried to quiet myself like my knight, but I couldn't still the tremble in my hand. The overpowering floral smell of the nicely appointed bathroom mixed poorly with my fear and turned my nearly empty stomach. Suddenly grateful I hadn't eaten much after our performance, I pressed my shaking hands into my stomach and tried not to retch bile.

After a moment, Geraint cracked the door and glanced up and down the hallway. Apparently satisfied with what he saw, he took my hand and pulled me after him. I didn't even mind, though his tight grip spoke of his fear and was not reassuring.

We found a side door. The wet humidity contrasted sharply with the conditioned air, and I shuddered at the abrupt change. It mixed with my fear, adding to the disconnect I felt with reality. Things like this did not happen. Hell, I didn't even know what this was. *Were we freaking out over nothing?*

A few path lights illuminated the dark night. Light filtered around the edges of drawn blinds from the house windows. Between the two, there was enough light to see the concrete sidewalk and avoid a few low-hanging branches from trees heavy with blossoms. The perfume of thousands of flowers clogged my nose.

Geraint picked up the pace, and I jogged behind him as we headed for the parking area where we'd left the van Robby should have our gear loaded in. He'd be waiting, possibly with the engine running. I was sure Geraint had already texted him, though I hadn't seen him do it.

When we'd arrived during the last bits of daylight, I'd found the grounds with their gardens and hedges and trees shielding the house from view of the rest of the neighborhood quite charming. Now I was jumping at shadows, expecting to get attacked at any moment.

There, the van, running, headlights shining down the driveway. Just a hundred more yards and we'd be on our way home.

Though I had been expecting an attack, when Geraint lunged forward, fist smacking into someone I hadn't even seen until they were sailing backward, I couldn't help but squeal in fear.

I'd never seen Geraint punch anything before, but the guy crumpled in the hedge certainly knew he'd been hit. Or he would when he woke up. *Damn.*

Geraint grabbed my arm, fingers bruisingly tight. I didn't complain, just ran with him. Hoping we'd make it.

We were almost there, close enough that I could see Robby in the driver's seat. Close enough that I could see him slumped over the steering wheel, when Geraint skidded to a halt, hands going up in the classic "don't shoot" pose.

He backed up, keeping between me and whoever held a gun on him. I assumed it was a gun, anyway.

"Give me a reason not to shoot you, knight," a voice said. "We don't need you."

No way. Not sure I comprehended what was going on, but pretty sure the guy meant they wanted me alive, I slipped around my knight and put myself in front of him.

"Ember," he hissed, trying to shove me behind him.

Geraint was strong, but I was far from weak, and I refused to budge. Unless he was going to pick me up, I was staying in front.

"What do you want?" I shouted.

The man who'd questioned us earlier at the party stepped out from the shadows. The two men in front of him held guns pointed at us. There was something weird about the guns, but I couldn't place what it was. All three of the men were entirely forgettable, especially in the uncertain lighting from the sparse illumination. Outside of vague impressions, I wouldn't even be able to describe them later. It was almost like they were imperfect clones of each other.

"You both come with us. If you don't resist, knight, you'll be able to continue your duties. If you fight us, we'll kill you and create another."

"I have no idea what you're talking about," Geraint said, but something about the tone of his musical lilt told me he knew exactly what these men referred to. I wasn't sure if they'd pick up on it, but I knew Geraint. I thought I did, anyway.

The men shared a look, and a fourth joined them from the direction we'd come from. Though he looked very much like the other three, blood smeared his face.

"He certainly hits like a knight," the man grumbled.

"Take them both. We'll sort it out later," the one that seemed to be in charge said. "If it's not them, then we'll keep looking and m'lord Baz will have more performers for his collection." The words were bitter and not at all pleased.

Whoever this Baz was, clearly these men weren't fans of his. The name tickled at my memory like a feather brushing at the back of my neck. I didn't have time to chase the feeling, though. Geraint's hands tightened on my arms, but there was nothing we could do against guns. I studied the weapons as they got closer, my vision narrowing until hands holding weapons were all I could focus on. Those seriously looked like ray guns from a seventies science-fiction show. *Were we getting abducted by aliens?* My sense of disconnect deepened. I didn't know a lot about firearms, but I was pretty sure they didn't make guns like that.

"You will come with us," the in-charge clone said.

Geraint sighed and kissed the top of my head. "We don't have an option right now."

I nodded.

"Leave your things," the man with the ray gun ordered.

My knight dropped our bags next to the driver's side door of the van we'd not quite made it to.

"If you have those portable phone things, leave them," the clone ordered.

Portable phone things? I knew he meant cell phones, but even someone who didn't speak English as a first language would know what they were called.

Mine was already in my bag. Geraint dropped his into his duffle and zipped it closed.

We were so screwed.

One of the two not obviously armed men grabbed me and jerked me forward. The armed men trained their guns on Geraint. It was an effective deterrent. I didn't want to get him shot, so I cooperated.

They dragged us back into the house by yet another side door. Maybe some sort of servant's entrance because the hallway, while still nice, was much plainer than anywhere else we'd been in the large mansion. The guy jerked me into something that looked like a ballroom or some sort of dance hall with a large mirror on one side.

Geraint sighed in resignation, but I had no idea what the hell they thought they were going to do with us in here.

The in-charge clone walked up to the mirror, putting his hand on it, and muttered something under his breath that I swore sounded like "Bloody Mary." He repeated the phrase three times.

I blinked, trying to wrap my mind around what new weird thing was happening, when something out of childhood nightmares and urban legend appeared in the mirror. White hair, sunken and glowing green eyes, high cheekbones, and lips pulled back in a desiccated grimace, revealing decaying teeth. The woman in the mirror wore a white dress and the hands she lifted were little more than skin-covered bones.

Whimpering, I glanced behind me, but no one fitting that description stood in the hall with us. No. This apparition only existed in the mirror.

"What the fuck?" I breathed.

"To the palace," the head clone said, sounding urgent and yet bored at the same time.

The woman in the mirror bowed and stepped back, revealing a translucent stone archway in the mirror.

In-charge clone stepped into the mirror, and he grew smaller as he walked through the archway.

"What the fuck?" I whispered again, an edge of panic making my voice fragile.

The clone with his hand clamped around my arm, dragged me forward. I screamed as he thrust me at the mirror, but instead of hard glass smashing my face, the feeling of cool liquid cradled my body, followed by my ears popping. I screamed for my knight.

Only cold, rushing air and silence answered.

CHAPTER 3

Ember

"What the fuck?" I whispered for the millionth time, arms clutched around my legs, hugging my knees to my chest as I rocked back and forth. The stone floor radiated its chill through my body, shivers wracking me and not entirely from fear. It was freaking cold in the small stone cage they'd thrown me in.

Everything was gray, from the blocks of stone making up the walls, to the bars on the front, to the hallway outside. Even my skin had taken on a gray tinge. That couldn't be healthy.

My brain had short-circuited when I'd stumbled out of the mirror into the cold, dry air of wherever the hell I was now. I'd glimpsed Geraint before I'd been dragged away, so I knew he'd also made the trip. Impressions of stone corridors and deep shadows, and a few precariously narrow and steep staircases, flitted through my memories before I'd been tossed in my cell. I had no idea where they'd taken Geraint.

Picking at the threads around the rip in my yoga pants, I fought tears and hoped the cut on my knee didn't get infected. Though, honestly, that was probably the least of my worries.

I needed to pee, but except for me, the cell was empty.

With no idea what else to do, I stood, nearly cracking my head on a low stone ceiling that had literally been shrouded in shadows. When I waved my hand through the air, the blackness swirled like smoke, except it clung to me in cool droplets. So maybe more akin to a shadowy fog?

Weird as hell.

The cell wasn't much taller than I was. I could stand, but if I stretched at all, I'd hit the top. Hunching my shoulders, I shuffled forward and sank down to the floor, so I didn't feel like the walls were closing in so much.

The bars were cold in my hands, like everything else. I pressed my face to the metal and looked around, trying to see up and down the hallway. The same black fog clung to the walls and the floors, shifting in an unfelt breeze.

I thought I saw other bars like the ones on the front of my cage up and down the hall, but the fog hid a lot of details. It was quiet down here, too. Even the sounds I made seemed muffled. Listening, I couldn't make out anything that made me think others inhabited those cells. No scents reached me except my sweat and a weird, dry papery smell. I expected dank mustiness, especially with the weird shadow fog, but it smelled dry.

Not sure what else to do, I was about to shout. The lack of anything but the sounds I made was making me feel a little crazy. Even negative attention was better than this.

While I tried to compose my first demands and force words from my lips, the air pressure changed and the slightest breeze tickled strands of my shoulder-blade-length hair. I wouldn't even have noticed if it weren't for the absolute stillness of the place.

The click of claws on hard ground displaced the silence and for a moment warmth pushed away the chill and the fear in my chest. The patter of paws on stone brought back fond memories of the pack of dogs I'd grown up with. Then the harshness of this strange reality crashed back down, and I whimpered as a version of the same heavy-jowled dogs I'd drawn by the lake a lifetime ago came into view. The pair padded toward me, red eyes locked on mine, lips drawn back to show gleaming white teeth. They were solid black, heavy bodied and broad shouldered like some sort of large bully breed dog. Drool leaked from their mouths and splattered on the floor. The black shadow fog swirled away from the dogs, but a small bit wasn't fast enough, and the drool landed on it, hissing like acid. The rest of the blackness fled, leaving the room feeling empty, even with the demonic dogs that had positioned themselves in front of my cell. They lowered themselves to their haunches and stared at me. One licked its lips as if hungry.

I winced in sympathy for the shadow stuff, though why I should feel any empathy for whatever that was, I didn't have a clue. Its absence left the room in a weird place lighting-wise. The ambient light was low but dispersed, and I had no idea where the illumination came from. The dogs did not seem to have shadows.

I held my hand out. My shadow was faint, but there. It still existed. For whatever reason I found that idea a tremendous relief. It wasn't like I was in Neverland, where I could lose my shadow.

Okay, so I didn't know that. I'd gone through a mirror to get here, after all. Still, getting to Neverland involved flying if I recalled correctly and I'd certainly not done any of that.

The dogs breathed heavily and filled the space with their presence. Despite being terrifying in appearance, it was nice not to be alone.

We stared at each other for a while. The only thing to mark the passage of time was the increasing pressure on my bladder and the dryness of my mouth.

I'd finally decided, again, to break the quiet and start yelling, when the unmistakable thud of boots on stone reached me.

My heart sped in my chest and anxiety increased the need to pee. *What now?* Whatever this was, I didn't want to meet it sitting on my ass, so I forced stiff knees to behave and climbed to my feet.

I didn't have to wait long before a man came into view. He wore some sort of uniform in shades of black and gray, blending in with the rest of the place. His skin was chalky. Not exactly Caucasian, more like someone had forgotten to shade in his features. He wore a sword at his hip, but the only color about the guy other than shades of gray was his pallid skin.

"Prince Baz will see you now." The guy's voice was as bland as the rest of him, lacking emotion and inflection.

"I need to use the restroom."

The guy gestured, and the bars in front of me dissolved into a gray mist. He didn't acknowledge my words, but I hoped that he'd understood.

I practically leaped out of the cell, as much as my legs—still tingling with pins and needles—would let me.

The dog creatures stood, quiet growls rumbling in their throats. I scooted away from them, hurrying after the guard when he turned and strode down the hallway. The dogs followed, and I imagined I could feel their hot pants on the back of my thighs. I couldn't, however, smell their breath.

We wound through narrow gray stone hallways. The initial surge of adrenalin faded, and my steps dragged, exhaustion tugging at my limbs and warring with fear for dominance in my body. I ached to have my knight at my side. Not knowing what had happened to him was worse than not knowing what was going on.

The hallway ended in a narrow stairway that seemed vaguely familiar, and I mentally tried to prepare myself for a long climb. My guard went up ahead of me and the dogs trailed behind, not able to go side by side in the narrow space. The ceiling was barely tall enough for the guard to walk upright. I could easily touch it if I wanted to put my arms over my head.

Worn valleys in the middle of the slick stone tripped up my feet, and I almost rolled my ankle. Falling was one of my bigger nightmares, ironic for an aerialist. Trembling with fear, I practically wept with joy when the guard pushed open a door set in the wall to the side of the stairs and ducked to step up through it. There was no landing, just continuous stairs upward and this door that allowed escape from the terror of a staircase.

The narrow hallway we squeezed through opened into another excessively gray corridor. This one was much larger, however.

I still couldn't tell where the light came from. It was about as bright as a full moon on a snowy landscape, except there was no obvious source of illumination. The shadowy fog was especially prevalent, cloaking the ceiling in mystery and shifting through the deep corners where there would normally be actual shadows.

Another door led into a bigger hall. This one, finally, had some color. A red runner down the middle, which my guide avoided walking on. Feeling contrary, I took to the center of the hall, and my feet sank into the thick carpet. It felt like some of my color bled back into me with the addition of the red to the landscape. My multi-colored sweater looked less gray, and the red in my yoga pants seemed to perk up. My skin no longer was a sickly gray, and the dried scab on my knee looked normal instead of washed out.

This was weird as fuck, not gonna lie, like I was in my own personal nightmare.

The dogs had no hesitation about following me onto the runner, but my guide continued to walk on the bare stone. Up ahead, more guards lined the walls. They all looked similar to the one who led me, though some were more female in appearance. Their skin tones ranged from chalky to black and every shade of gray in between. They were clearly not human.

They all held some sort of weapon and stood at attention, unnaturally still. I saw their eyes flick toward me then straight ahead, though they could almost have been decorations. *So creepy.* They all had flat gray eyes that reminded me distantly of Geraint's. His were anything but flat, however. No, his stormy gray eyes were full of vibrant life.

My skin crawled, and I pressed my hands against my stomach, though not too tightly, as I really had to pee.

Two of the weird not-human guards stood at a set of large doors at the end of the hallway. These also had color, a rich brown, banded with straps that looked iron. The guards dragged open the doors, and my guide walked through. I followed since the dog creatures still pressured me from behind.

We entered some sort of chamber where the only place to sit in the entire room other than the floor was a throne sitting on an elevated stage. Three other thrones still sat on the dais but lay knocked onto their sides. The room itself was the same unrelieved shades of gray with shadow lurking everywhere. Stone pillars lined the hall, but nothing adorned the walls. Rich red fabric padded the standing throne, contrasting with the dark wood. I wouldn't be surprised if the others were similar.

Interesting.

"Kneel here." The guard pointed to a spot in front of the empty stage.

I stood where the guard had said to kneel. He stared at me impassively. I glared back.

"Stand down. She'll be on her knees soon enough," a deeply resonant voice said, approaching from the side.

Anger pushed away my fear. What a fucking dick thing to say. Aware that I was in a precarious position, I kept my mouth shut, but I wanted to give whoever spoke a piece of my mind.

"Your Highness." My guard bowed and stepped away. The dog creatures went with him, leaving me alone in the middle of the room while the owner of the offensive words came toward me.

If I didn't already hate this Baz guy, I'd have found him very handsome. The normalcy of his appearance contrasted sharply with all the gray-scale people. He had rich mahogany brown skin and short-cropped black hair. He was taller than me by several inches, broad shouldered, and had a fantastic voice. The only thing odd about this guy were his gray eyes. *Did everyone here have gray eyes?* Unlike the guards' his were not flat gray and contained depths of life. The cruel smile on his face stole any warmth I might have felt toward someone who at least looked human. He dressed in a black suit with crisp lines and a deep red tie over a black dress shirt. Not a lot of color, but the tie stood out after all the gray.

"Hello, Princess," the guy said.

I glared. "Where the hell am I?"

He turned, hands clasped behind his back, and stalked around me, studying me. "You, my dear, are now in the Dream Realm, and here you will remain."

"No, I won't," I replied firmly. "I will go home, and where is Geraint? He's going home with me."

Baz—this had to be the Prince Baz asshole the guard had mentioned—chuckled. "You're a mortal, and you've come to Dream. You're bound to this realm now."

I wanted to argue, but much like with his name, a fragment of a memory tickled at me. I wanted to brush the feathery feeling away from my mind, but it wasn't a physical thing to push away. Something about what he was saying reminded me of a story from my childhood. What? I had no idea.

"We are looking for our princess. Perhaps you are she?" He seemed to ask me to confirm I was this princess, but something told me there wasn't going to be a fairytale ending if I was, so I kept my mouth shut.

"Time will tell. Until then, you'll entertain us."

"What?" I blurted out.

"In my search for our Princess, I've amassed quite a collection of dreambound performers. It's become a hobby of mine to watch them. I'm told you are quite talented."

He waved his hand, and a black set of silks tumbled from the darkness above. "Perform," he ordered.

"No."

He raised his eyebrows, and the smile that hadn't left his lips deepened. "I like to play with my toys, Princess. Keep that in mind. The more willing you are, the sooner I'll lose interest."

"Fuck you."

That pulled a chuckle out of him. "If nothing else, it will be entertaining to break you."

I shivered, ignoring the silks that dangled behind me.

He stepped forward, invading my personal space and pressing something sharp against my throat. "Get in the air, now."

"Same answer," I replied, staring straight ahead. He could only kill me once, after all. Something told me he wasn't ready to go that far, anyway, which made me a little bolder than I might otherwise have been.

"Sir," someone outside of my field of view said. The voice sounded familiar. Maybe one of the jerks who had kidnapped me and Geraint? "She values the knight."

Definitely one of those jerks. Damn them.

The sharp edge left my neck. "Bring him."

I wanted to see Geraint, but I didn't want him used to persuade me. "Look, I gotta pee. Then maybe I can climb for you."

Prince Baz turned a disdainful look my way. "You can take care of your human concerns later."

"When I get in the air, the silks will press on my stomach. My bladder is full. I'll probably pee all over myself and your fancy silks."

The absolute lack of concern on the prince's face chilled me. I wasn't even sure he actually understood what the issue was.

Before I could elaborate, two gray beings dragged my knight into the room. The contrast between him and them couldn't have been starker. He was full of colors and life. They were gray and flat.

He struggled when he saw me, eyes wide, though I could read the relief in his expression. Bright purple bruising swelled one of his eyes shut, and a crust of blackish red flakes marred the golden stubble on his jaw where he'd bled, probably from his nose. Or maybe he had a split lip. I couldn't tell.

The gray beings shoved Geraint to his knees. One pulled his head back by his hair and the other put his sword to my knight's throat.

I absolutely believed they'd kill him if I didn't cooperate. Damn it all.

"Having a weakness is the pits, isn't it?" Prince Baz said, voice mild. "Now, dance for us, Princess."

Praying they wouldn't hurt Geraint, and praying that I wouldn't piss myself while in the air, I rubbed the sweat off my hands on my pants, and awkwardly bent over to take off my shoes and socks. I doubted I'd have time to stretch or get more appropriate clothing, since they wouldn't even let me relieve myself, so I just hoped I didn't strain any cold muscles too much.

I stared up at the silks, wondering what they were attached to, in no way thinking I was safe, but hoping they wouldn't want to break me or kill me just yet.

Geraint hissed in pain.

"Don't keep me waiting," Baz warned.

Muttering curses under my breath, I rubbed my palms on my thighs again and flexed my hands, trying to wake up my cold, tired muscles at least a little. Adrenalin was a great temporary boost, but I'd pay for it later.

I took the silks in my hand, then jerked away at the cold, clingy feeling. Had they formed from the shadow fog? Did they attach to anything?

My knight took a deeper breath, and I knew they'd hurt him again, though he'd tried to hide his reaction from me.

Not having any choice, I reached up, gripped the fabric, and lifted, twisting my feet into the silks and pushing myself higher. I climbed until I was just under the ceiling of black fog, then I inverted, crocheting my legs into the silks. Tightening my stomach, I lifted myself into the air, grabbed the silks over my knees, and pulled myself up until I was sitting with the fabric wrapped around my thighs, just under my hips.

Normally I loved setting up for a drop, the sensual climb of dancing up the silks, the burn of my muscles as I twisted my body in ways most people never even imagined, wrapping the fabric around my body, pushing myself as I put on a show. Today, I completed the moves and wraps for the drop with little grace and no enthusiasm. I had no idea if Baz would know the difference or not, but I just couldn't bring myself to put on a show any more than I already was. Maybe it was the lack of music. Naw, had to be the kidnapping and death threats. That was a total mood killer.

My setup for the drop complete, I threw myself into it, expecting the silks to snap tight around my body and stop my fall.

Instead, they vanished, and I plummeted toward the ground. I didn't even have time to scream before something tightened around my ankle, jerking me to a stop with my head inches from the floor. I could feel the cold radiating from the hard stone.

Sounds filtered through my shock, Geraint shouting in anger, someone laughing their ass off, a few angry grunts as someone hit someone else.

I just stared at the floor shaking, warm liquid soaking my yoga pants. I needed Geraint's arms around me, but he didn't come. Instead, polished black shoes came into my view.

"Oh, we are going to have so much fun together, little dove," Baz cooed. "So much fun."

CHAPTER 4

Ember

They'd given me a room that was only better than the cell had been because it had rudimentary bathroom facilities. I'd stripped my clothing and left it in a sodden heap in one corner and gotten into the shower despite the icy chill of the water. *Was nothing warm here?*

Pressing my hand against the stone wall, I wished for a hot water and soap. Slowly, my shivers subsided as the chill left the liquid streaming from the wall. Twin nightmares plagued me while I stood under the water, the vanishing silks and the freefall through the air, and the horror image of my knight being dragged away, unconscious, a streak of red trailing out behind him and bringing some color to the unrelieved grayness of the place.

I didn't know if he was still alive, and sadly, focusing on that was preferable to dwelling on my other fear. The silks had vanished. They'd betrayed me, dropping me and Geraint hadn't been able to catch me.

My fingers clenched into fists without me telling them to, digging nails into my palms. I pressed my knuckles into the stone and tried to quiet my trembles, to keep the scream that was just on the other side of my lips from escaping. If I let it out, I might never stop.

When I finally got out of the lukewarm water, my clothing had vanished. I had planned to wash it and wear it dry, but now that choice was taken from me. Were they going to leave me naked, then?

I squeezed a little of the water out of my hair and stepped from the shower. I hadn't even checked for a towel, not that I would have stayed covered in piss and sweat and fear when there was an option to get clean.

The water dripped off me, splatting on the stone floor, loud enough to drown out the silence, and I was grateful for it. I almost turned the stream of water back on just to have some noise, but finally refrained and dripped my way out into the small bedroom area.

A black robe lay on the small, hard mat, probably intended to be a bed. *Well, that was better than nothing*, I supposed. This time, the weird damp, clingy feeling of the fabric didn't shock me. Raising my eyebrows, I held it up. I'd thought it was a robe or a blanket, but it was a dress.

The thing adjusted to fit me perfectly when I slipped it on. Like, no joke, just shrunk right up, covering me but also form fitting. I was instantly a hundred times warmer, too. Well, whoever had left that for me had at least left me something good.

"Thank you," I breathed, the grateful words displacing the scream I hadn't yet voiced and buried it deeply for use another time. I had no idea if anyone would hear my gratitude, even so, it helped me to say it.

I rubbed the fabric on my arms. It no longer felt cold and clingy, more like a nice jersey cotton, but tougher somehow. For now, this would work well enough. I didn't wear a lot of dresses outside of gigs, but it was just another kind of costume right now.

Exhausted, I lay down on the pad, expecting it to be hard and uncomfortable. Like the dress, it surprised me, molding to my body and warming quickly. I didn't have a blanket, but someone or something answered my wish to be clothed and warmer, at least. It was the little things.

Those thoughts and worry for Geraint chased me into a fitful sleep broken by dreams and nightmares like I hadn't had since I was a child.

***

My stomach woke me some time later. Licking my dry lips, I glanced around. Nothing had changed in the room. The lighting was the same strange, diffused illumination from an unknown source. The same shadows clung to the walls and swirled along the ceiling. Still, it felt different, and I wasn't sure what I was experiencing until I realized the air temperature was comfortable.

Huh.

I got up, stretching sore and abused muscles, ignoring the twinges I'd normally take the time to work out. My usual stretching routine was so far from what I wanted to be doing that I skipped it, heading into the bathroom and taking care of my needs. I drank water out of the sink. That helped some of my hunger, but it wasn't really enough. I hadn't eaten a decent meal since brunch a lifetime ago.

Shit, I hadn't even thought about Robby. Remembering his slumped form in our van, I hoped he was okay. I spared a passing thought for my little succulent plant, but as much as I loved the thing, that was the least of my worries right now.

Somewhat refreshed, I went out into the bedroom area of the cell. A tray of food had appeared while I was gone. Curious, I tried the door, but as with every other time I'd tried to tug the iron ring to open the door, it didn't budge.

The food itself looked like some sort of simple meat sandwich. Like, someone had taken Wonder Bread, slapped some American cheese on it along with some ham,

47

and I hoped that was mayo and not the other crap people used as a condiment. Weird as hell, but I wasn't going to complain about any food at this point. While I wondered if it was safe to eat, they really didn't need to poison me to get me to cooperate. They just had to put a knife to Geraint's throat, and I'd do about anything they wanted. I took a cautious bite. It tasted exactly like it looked like it should, and I woofed it down. None of that was food I'd normally eat, but it helped to fill the void.

After I'd eaten, I sat and stared at the door. And I stared some more. Nothing happened. For whatever reason, I'd thought they'd pay more attention to me. If I was supposed to be this princess, wouldn't they want to test me? To find out?

Of course, simply being ignored might be better. Safer anyway. At least in the short term.

After another eternity of staring at the door didn't produce any sort of change, I sighed. May as well do some of my stretches. My body ached and I could work some of it out, anyway. I wasn't used to long periods of being still and despite the lingering hunger, restlessness had me folding my hands and fiddling with the hem of the dress I wore.

I stood, and the dress shifted with my intention, encasing my legs and turning into some sort of full body cat suit.

"Okay, that's cool as shit," I muttered. At least something down here seemed to like me, even if it was a piece of shadow clothing.

I exercised until I was as loose as I was going to get after abusing my body. Then I sat on the mat and tried to figure out what to do. When I jerked my eyelids open one too many times, I lay back and let myself sleep. I had no answers and no reason not to nap.

With no way to mark time, and no actual change in my environment, I couldn't tell the passing of time. Meals were sporadic, though I noticed a pattern after a few cycles of sleep. If I dreamed about food, the quality of what appeared in my room would be vastly better than if I didn't. After that, I tried to think about what I'd like my next meal to be before I fell asleep. Whoever was reading my dreams and preparing my food didn't always get it right, but after I discovered I could influence them, the meals were a lot better than the first attempt to feed me. They'd even managed chocolate cake, once.

With nothing else to do to amuse myself, it became some sort of game. See if I could dream what I wanted for my next meal. I also tried dreaming about Geraint, but that, unfortunately, didn't produce the same sort of results. Those dreams just left me feeling empty and lonely, or horny and lonely, not to mention worried about my knight. My dreams, and learning to change the appearance of my clothing, were my only amusements outside of exercise.

I needed my knight, but I remained completely alone, the only sounds ones I made or the running water I sometimes left on just to have some noise. Even listening at the door produced nothing.

Finally, I started drawing on the walls with the shadow stuff. Landscapes, memories of home, using my fingers and the shadow to paint the walls. Then I erased it all like some sort of Etch-A-Sketch.

I started to understand why solitary isolation was such a harsh punishment.

Days must have passed before the door finally swung inward.

Eyes wide, I stared, covering my mouth with my hand, afraid to speak.

My knight glanced around the room before slipping inside and shutting the door behind him.

49

I threw myself into his arms, and he held me close. Geraint was shirtless, and old and new bruises yellowed and blackened his normal tan. That and his hollowed cheeks and wide eyes told me he'd fared much worse than I had.

"Geraint, what is going on?" I sobbed, tears coating my cheeks.

He held me tightly, rocking me. "I don't have time to explain," he whispered. "I have to go before they figure out I'm not in the cell they left me in."

"But—"

"Shhh, it'll be okay, Spark. Listen, tonight Prince Baz has arranged a show with all his performers that he's taken over the years. They'll come get you, obviously. Do what they tell you. Don't fight them."

"But—"

"This is important, Ember. Just cooperate. Act beaten. At the end of the show, you'll have a chance to escape. Others will help you. I'll cause a distraction and you just run. Find Prince Nic. I won't make it out, but you must go."

"I'm not leaving you, Geraint."

He sighed and rested his cheek against my head. "I don't want you to leave me, but you have to. There is more at stake than just you and me. Prince Nic can tell you everything you need to know once you're safe. They probably won't kill me, Spark. So, you know, maybe you can rescue me." He said the last playfully.

"Yeah, I'll do that." He was joking. I was serious. If there was a way, I'd find it. Probably a little optimistic, considering I still had no idea where I was. "You are sure there's no way for both of us to escape?"

"If I can get away, I will, but I don't think both of us will get out, and you have to."

"But if you escape, you can rescue me," I replied, trying to keep the tears out of my voice and failing.

"I am rescuing you, Spark. Right now. Act broken, escape tonight when the opportunity presents. Promise me you'll run. It's our only chance."

Swallowing the sobs trying to escape, I nodded and rubbed at my nose.

"One last thing. Be sure to tell Prince Nic that Baz didn't recognize you. That's important, and he needs to know."

"Why—?"

"If I answer that question, I'll be here answering more and more questions and we'll get caught. Prince Nic will tell you everything. I love you, Spark."

Geraint wiped a tear from my cheek, then pressed his lips to mine.

Before I could clutch him against me and deepen the kiss, the door opened, and Geraint jerked back as if not wanting to get caught kissing me.

"We must go, knight. The Princess agrees?" It was one of the weird gray people, though this one had a bit more animation in his eyes than most.

"She does," Geraint replied, fixing me with a stare.

Slowly, I nodded. I'd do what he said. I'd find this Nic guy and then I'd rescue Geraint. I just hoped Nic wasn't as much of a douche canoe as Baz was.

Though I wanted to scream and throw a giant tantrum when the door *thunked* shut behind Geraint, instead I sat on the mat on the floor and wondered how long it would be until I had to put on a show. Could I do it? Could I act beaten?

Then I remembered the bruises covering my knight's body. If I didn't, they'd take my disobedience out on Geraint. So, yes, I could put on this performance. I would do it for Geraint, and then I would escape for him, and I

51

would come back. I didn't care what Prince freaking Baz said. Once I had my knight back, we were returning home.

***

I shifted my shadow clothing to the black cat suit most appropriate to a silks performance and attempted to limber up. After that, I sat and tried to calm myself. I'd drifted back to sleep when someone pounded on the door.

My heart leaped into my throat and adrenalin flooded my system. I scrambled to my feet in a rush, tripping over myself in my haste, but managing not to sprawl into a heap. Two of the gray men waited outside, swords at their hips. They had the completely flat gray eyes I'd mostly come to expect.

"You will come with us," one intoned emotionlessly.

Anger surged, but I forced myself to recall Geraint's bruises. He certainly hadn't said anything about them, but I knew at least some wounds were my fault.

Dropping my gaze to the stone floor, I nodded. If nothing else, at least I was getting out of the room.

Meek as a mouse, I followed. The difference in air temperature from my cell to the hallway sucked the air from my lungs and my toes curled against the frigid stone. They hadn't returned my shoes.

With a quick thought, my shadow clothing crawled across my feet and covered them like slippers. That helped, and I unwrapped my arms from my body.

They led me through yet another gray stone corridor, but this time we came to a set of iron-banded heavy wooden doors I hadn't seen yet. They pushed the doors open. I couldn't help but stop on the other side and stare.

Nothing had truly convinced me I was no longer on Earth until I stepped outside.

The sky was black, as if it were night, but no stars shone above, and no moon. It was as if the sky was filled with the same weird shadow mist that lined the castle or whatever it was I'd been in. I turned and looked. Yep, some sort of crumbly castle thing complete with crenellations and vicious cracks that made me think someone had attacked the place, and they'd never bothered to repair it.

The dry, dusty smell of the first cell I'd woken in was stronger here, tickling my nose and provoking a quick sneeze. The lighting was the same weird, pervasive illumination. I was becoming used to it, but that didn't mean I didn't miss the sun.

The land existed in shades of gray and black, though some places lightened almost to white. The scenery was stark, trees black of bark and bare of leaves. The ground looked to be some sort of dark gray gravel material. Was there any freaking color in this place? Other than the occasional splash of red? I shied away from my memory of the smear of blood Geraint had left when they'd dragged him away. Fortunately, I knew he was alive, but after tonight? He might not survive my escape attempt. I might not either.

I really needed to not focus on that.

They had laid out a circus tent in shades of black and gray in a large courtyard in front of the castle. Creatures—I could only describe them as creatures—streamed into the tent. Great… a circus. I loved performing, but these circumstances were crap.

The gray men let me gawk for a few minutes, but then they started forward down massive stone steps. I scrambled after them, trying to keep up the pretense that I was cowed.

Some creatures turned and looked at me. A few gazes lingered past mere interest. I couldn't read any of the emotions in their faces, but if I had to guess, it was curiosity. Many of the beings were humanoid at least, but most of them were oddly proportioned, skeletal, had extra appendages, or were otherwise obviously not human. Not to mention the shades of gray everyone exhibited. Like, these creatures should have been terrifying, but they came across as flat, much like the guards in the palace.

Here and there a set of eyes sparked with a bit more life, and those were the gazes that lingered. I should have been afraid, but I just felt sad. Something told me those gazes weren't supposed to be flat and lifeless. Those creatures should have been animated enough to instill fear even in me. Even in me? Where had that thought come from? Of course I should be afraid.

Still, I couldn't shake the feeling that things weren't right, despite having nothing to base that feeling on.

My guards led us around the side of the tent and in through the back. The tent itself didn't seem as if it would hold the numbers of beings flowing into the entrance. We came into a backstage area. There they left me.

In general, I knew what to do. Even if I hadn't had Geraint's warning, it would have been obvious they wanted me to perform. I cast my gaze about, looking for a clue as to where I should go, or if I could get away. A quick glance back at the entrance showed the two guards standing outside the split in the canvas. Now clearly wasn't the time for me to attempt escape. Geraint had said after the performance.

Heart pounding in my chest, I took a deep breath and moved farther into the space. The ground had taken on the consistency of packed dirt instead of the gravel stuff I'd walked across before. The lighting back here was even lower than in the rest of whatever hell I was currently in, and I squinted as I looked around. The black fog hung heavily in here, but I didn't want to walk blindly into it.

"Oh, there you are."

I jumped, spinning around. A girl skipped out of the fog. At first, all I could take in was the vibrant color of her leotard. Even in the dim light, the swirling yellows and blues were dazzling after not seeing any color other than red for so long. Once I looked beyond the sparkly colors of her outfit, I focused on her face. She wore stage makeup, which made it a little harder to guess her age. Maybe sixteen? She had a dancer's body, shorter, lithe, and lean, but well-muscled. Her eyes were a light brown and not at all flat, like maybe she was real?

I remembered what Geraint said about others, that Baz had captured other circus performers.

"I'm Ember," I said after a flustered moment.

"Yeah, we know. The latest 'princess.'" She said the last with a bit of sarcasm. "I'm Paige."

"What is going on?" I hoped she would give me more information than my knight had.

"Every once in a while, Prince Baz remembers he has us, especially when he captures another potential princess. Then he drags us out to perform for the masses."

"But, why? I don't understand."

"Neither do we. Not really. The little we've been able to figure out is pretty obvious. Baz is looking for his long-lost princess and he thinks she's some sort of entertainer focusing on the circus arts. We don't exactly know why he wants his princess, because he fucking hates all of us. I think he wants to kill her." She said the last with a shrug. "At least he decided I wasn't it. I'm stuck here now, but it's not too bad until he remembers he has us. Come on. We don't have a ton of time to get ready." Paige pushed through the curtain of black fog. I followed, mostly used to the damp, clingy feeling now.

We came out into a dressing room of sorts. The mirrors were all shattered, but some pieces were big enough that people could see their faces to apply theater makeup. Several women were in various stages of preparing for the show. Some seemed to be about Paige's age, while the oldest was probably in her late twenties.

I hadn't been around anyone but myself for a while, and the presence of other humans brought tears to my eyes. I blinked them away and took a deep breath. Scents other than the weird dry dustiness I'd grown able to ignore were especially pungent. The sharp scents of makeup, the smell of other people's sweat, and a distant aroma of—was that popcorn?—nearly overwhelmed me before I adapted.

Paige rattled off a series of names I didn't catch. "My act is second to last," Paige said, breaking through my shocked reaction to the others. "You're last."

"Okay. What am I doing?"

She shrugged. "Don't know, what's your specialty?"

"Aerial silks or straps."

"Probably one of those, then." She didn't seem too concerned.

I shuddered, remembering how the silks had vanished. Could I get back in the air knowing that could happen again? Would I have a choice? Geraint had said to cooperate, act beaten, but would the fabric vanishing and sending me plummeting to the ground break me? If the ground didn't, that was. If Baz hated us, he might simply choose not to save me from splattering on the ground.

"Here, get ready." She shoved me at one of the broken mirrors. Makeup formed from the shadows, ready for me to apply. "And change your outfit to something shinier."

"It does something other than black?"

Paige shrugged.

Frowning, I focused on a light pastel swirl of green and purple with gold highlights.

The weird shadow outfit I wore hesitated—that was the only way I could describe the weird sensation I felt—then it seemed to shrug just as Paige had, and shifted.

The girl next to me gasped.

"Oh, shit." Paige stared. They all stared. "I meant from the costumes." She pointed at a rack along the far wall I hadn't noticed with my focus on the other humans.

"Oh."

"Shit," Paige repeated. "You're her, aren't you? They really found you."

"I honestly have no idea. None of you can make the shadow stuff change?"

They shook their heads.

"Well, you're screwed," Paige replied, seeming to dismiss her shock and move on to preparing for the show.

"That's nice." I sighed.

"Yeah, we think he wants to kill the princess because we've heard that some sort of dark nothingness is eating away at the edges of Dream, and it will go away if it gets the princess. Or some shit like that. So probably a sacrifice."

I swallowed, then caught a hint of movement out of the corner of my eyes. "How long have you all been here?" I changed the subject.

"Forever. Impossible to tell. Nothing changes, except sometimes another one of us shows up, and then we have to do all of this. You'll get used to it, eventually. Unless he kills you." She waved her hand at the backstage area. Her tone changed, and I thought she might have caught sight of whoever lurked in the shadows, too. "Then the prince forgets about all of us again for a while. Now finish your makeup."

Falling silent and trying to ignore the furtive glances from the others, I got to work on my face. Years of practice had me ready in short order.

57

Then we warmed up in the small backstage area, not saying much. I wanted to know more, but we were being observed and I didn't want to make it any more obvious that I might actually be their princess than I already had. I still didn't understand how that was possible, but maybe this Nic guy could fill me in. If I escaped. And it sounded like we really were in the dream world. Maybe I could rescue these women, too. It sounded like they'd been taken because of me. Clearly it wasn't my fault. Even so, if I could help, I would. What kind of psycho kidnapped people because he was looking for someone specific?

Geraint's insistence that I tell this Prince Nic guy that Baz hadn't recognized me filtered back into my thoughts. I was missing so many pieces of the puzzle. My mind churned over the possibilities while I went through my warmup routine on autopilot.

Not coming up with any answers, I brought my focus back to the present. I might not survive tonight, but I didn't want my death to happen because I was distracted.

The familiar burn of muscles as I stretched and warmed them up helped center me. The other women warmed up in near silence, their breathing coming in heavier gasps and the thud of feet hitting the ground as they jogged in place, or a soft grunt as they did pushups, were the only real sounds. Sweat odor mixed with the pervasive dusty smell.

Music struck up out front and the women froze, eyes going wide. The strains of a familiar song teased my ears, but instead of comforting, the sound sent tingles of disquiet through me. The music was familiar, but not quite right. It was as if an inept band played the song, but it wasn't just that the occasional cord was wrong, or some note blown too hard. No, it was as if all of that had happened, and the music had simply shifted somehow. I couldn't put my finger on it, but I could see why the others were disturbed.

I hoped it was simply the weirdness to the music that had them upset, and not some other sort of special torture.

Still, they didn't speak, and our unseen observers lurked in the shadows, so I didn't ask.

One of the flat gray people came back from the stage area. This one looked more feminine, with rounded curves and the suggestion of breasts.

"First act," she barked.

The women seemed to have a set order, and I'd been told to go last, so I finished my stretches as one of the girls closer to my age went onto the stage.

I heard no clapping, no sounds from the audience, and no announcer. That, by itself, was a nightmare for a performer.

Glancing around the edge of the curtain, I saw the woman standing on a large gray ball and juggling while she rolled around. She wore a gold sequined costume that would have looked fantastic under proper stage lighting. The audience stared vacantly like a class of uncaring students with an especially boring teacher. The performer was fantastic, but no one seemed to care. Not that I hadn't had an idea of why they might not want to get on stage before, but I was getting an idea of how bad this really was going to be.

For Geraint. I could do it for Geraint.

Time dragged, and each woman came back from their act, looking defeated. The others crowded around, assuring her she'd done well, but even to me, their words sounded hollow.

Finally, it was Paige's turn. She shot me an indecipherable look before she headed onto the stage. By the props waiting for her, she had some sort of gymnastic bars routine.

I watched, but it was the same. She performed brilliantly, but no one made a sound. The music stayed constant through the entire show, the disturbing, not quite right song on repeat, as if it were the only notes the band knew. Maybe that was the case.

Paige finished, bowed, and left the stage.

Her apparatus vanished into a cloudy mist and silks dropped from the top of the tent. They ended in the ever-present black fog, and I suspected they weren't actually real or attached to anything.

Wishing for a crash mat or a way to avoid this, I took a breath and steeled myself.

"Word of advice," Paige whispered. "Despite the lame audience, dance as if your life depends on it."

She didn't need to elaborate, and I nodded sharply once before going onto the stage. I took a moment to scan the crowd. Geraint wasn't among the beings I could see. *Was the escape plan still on?*

"I believe our new princess needs some instruction on how these shows work," a cold, familiar voice said, and Prince Baz stepped out of the shadows, dragging my knight with him.

Geraint gave me a quick nod before Baz threw him to the ground.

"You will entertain me, or I'll find a way to make your act more interesting." He grinned at me.

I shuddered and headed for the dangling silks. The familiar wet, clingy material stretched only a little as I grabbed with my hands and wrapped my feet, climbing slowly. I tried for sensual, but the best I could do was functional as I made my way up. It was surprisingly difficult to come up with a move to do. My brain blanked, and I simply couldn't process anymore.

Not sure what else to do, I hung from my arms, scissored my legs around the silks and folded over into a hip key. This gave me some room to think, hanging sideways from where the fabric wrapped around my hips. I grabbed the tails and twirled them, putting me into a spin. Trying to get into the mood, I danced through a few shapes while I hung there, increasing and decreasing the rate of my turn.

"Unacceptable," Baz said, and the silks freaking vanished.

My heart leaped into my throat, and I yelped as I fell. Anger burned through my fear. If I splattered on the ground, I didn't want my last emotion to be panic, and he'd done this to me before.

Sure enough, tendrils of shadow snagged my limbs before I hit the ground, jerking my body, and threatening to give me whiplash.

"Try again." His bored tone threatened more of the same.

Unacceptable, my ass. It wasn't an advanced move, but I'd like to see him get up there and do any of what I'd just done.

I had a feeling Baz simply didn't appreciate aerial silks. Or he wanted to torture me. I wasn't sure. Maybe he was hoping for a repeat of the first time he'd dropped me. I felt too numb, despite the anger, to give him the show he wanted. Maybe he'd just decide to be done with me and not catch me. Then Geraint could escape, and I wouldn't have to worry about it any longer. I shook out my arms and legs, ignoring the pain in my shoulders from the rough handling.

The silks dangled in front of me. I glanced over at the prince and my knight. Fury darkened Geraint's eyes. His lips were drawn back from his teeth, but the sword to his back had the appropriate impact, and he stayed put on the ground.

Clenching my jaw, I climbed again, this time making it a little fancier and trying to dance up the silks like I normally would. There was a point when I'd enjoyed this, but it seemed like several lifetimes ago.

I didn't even get halfway before the silks vanished. The shriek that escaped my mouth was probably the entertainment Baz was after, but another fear washed through me. They could break me and still sacrifice me. I doubted "limbs intact" was a requirement. The possibility of being broken scared me more than the genuine threat to my life.

This time, I almost hit the ground before my ribs groaned in protest as shadows wrapped around my waist and yanked me upward.

From the expression on Geraint's face, he might have come to the same conclusion. I shook my head and tried to work the fear out of my system. My hands shook as I reached for the reformed silks.

I almost couldn't even make the basic climb work, but Baz let me get almost to the top before he dropped me. This time, I curled into a ball like a diver and insured that if I hit the ground, it would probably end me.

The tendrils of shadow caught me farther off the ground this time. Baz knew I was on to him. Unlike last time, the shadows didn't lower me to the ground. I was tempted to push my power against his, but that would be a dead giveaway that I was the alleged princess he was after—emphasis on the dead. Or, at least, it would tell him I had some control over my environment here. I still didn't believe I was this dream princess.

The shadow stuff spun me, but I was used to that and simply waited. Right now, I was trapped. In the next moment? Who knew?

"You're very disappointing, Princess," Baz said. "I thought you'd be more fun. The other princesses are at least wise enough to entertain me."

I remained quiet, taking deep breaths, trying to keep the panic at bay. A tiny voice in the back of my mind screamed every swear word I knew, and I let it handle all the fear, while I kept my stage persona as intact as I could manage.

"Perhaps I should take my displeasure out on this knight. You seem to care about it."

Geraint's shoulders lifted with a sharp breath, but otherwise he gave no indication that he felt anything.

I squeezed my eyes shut, tears leaking through my lids and dampening my cheek. The salty water moistened my dry lips, and I clenched them tight, trying to trap in any sounds I might make.

"Sir," I heard a male voice whisper. "The cryptids are attacking."

Instead of acting worried, Baz sighed in irritation. "Again?"

"This force is considerably larger than the last incursion."

The prince let out a dramatic sigh and spun on his heels. "Deal with that." He pointed at Geraint.

The shadows didn't dissipate, but I thought I could handle them. Clearly, Baz thought he'd leave me hanging, literally. Anger pushed away the fear one more time.

"You heard your Prince, to arms!" One of the gray people shouted.

The crowd shuffled, sounding like a flutter of paper in a light breeze as they silently filed out of the tent. That was weird as shit. Also, though I smelled popcorn, I didn't see any.

"Geraint!" I shouted, but he was already being dragged away. I thought the gray person who'd brought him to me was the one who had his hand around my knight's arm, but I couldn't be sure.

"Shit," I muttered and focused on the shadow stuff holding me suspended. It no longer answered to Baz, as he'd simply left it. However, it didn't have any reason to respond to me, either. The clothing I wore had days to get used to me manipulating it, as did the shadow stuff in my cell. This piece of fog ignored my pleading attempts to get it to release me.

Finally, in a fit of desperation, I shoved everything I had at the unresponsive strands, hoping to force it to listen.

It dissipated, and I had a half second to realize my mistake before I plummeted toward the ground.

I landed hard. Nothing broke, but my shoulder took the brunt of the fall. I didn't think I'd dislocated it, but it hurt like hell.

"Fuck," I cried, tears blurring my vision.

Blinking them away, I saw my chance. The other women stared at me from backstage, but I couldn't do anything to help them. Not yet. Maybe this Nic guy could help. One of the shadow people came toward me. I bolted. They would not catch me again.

CHAPTER 5

Ember

The flaps of the tent slapped against me as I fled from the relatively calm interior into the chaos outside. My colorful clothing drew immediate attention.

"Shit," I muttered and forced the material into mottled blacks and grays, flowing some of it over my feet to protect me as I ran.

I still drew attention, but not nearly as much.

A few of the gray people shouted, but the attackers had their attention. They had my attention, too. Beasts out of legend charged out of the mists, swinging clubs, swords, knives. In some cases, they fought with bow and arrow or other projectiles. Large, hairy creatures that reminded me of Bigfoot charged past.

Wolves howled in the distance, and a few gigantic canines raced ahead of the Bigfoot charge. Men wearing ski masks and wielding blades, and—*oh god, was that a creepy-ass doll with a knife?*

I screamed and ran.

The shadowy mist swallowed me, muffling the sounds of the fight and hiding me from view. It also hid everything else, and it wasn't long before I plowed into a tree.

Screaming in pain as my wrist bent backward and rough bark scraped my forearms, I sank to the ground. I couldn't run blindly, but I couldn't stay here.

Command the mists, a quiet voice whispered to me.

Was it my voice? Was it someone else's? I didn't know and didn't care.

If only it were that easy.

Fighting sobs and rubbing at tears, I gasped for breath and tried to convince the shadows to make a path so I could see.

The mists parted, far easier than the shadow stuff that had held me suspended above the ground.

It took me a minute to react, but then I scrambled to my feet and forced my aching limbs to propel me forward. If I hurt now, I couldn't imagine how I'd feel when the adrenalin wore off.

I ran as long as I could, isolated from the fighting by my shadowy fog bank. The sounds of conflict faded behind me, and I hoped the cryptids weren't hurt too badly attacking Baz and his minions.

Through the fog of my fear, I noticed that the surrounding landscape had changed. The sky lightened to a not quite blueish gray, the foliage had not quite brown and not quite green tints to it over the ever-present gray-scale, and here and there a patch of color shone through the shades of gray. *Interesting.*

I stumbled along, trying to keep going, but not sure how long I could, or should, continue. *How will I find this Nic guy? Does he know I'm looking for him?* So many questions, and I had no answers.

Finally, unable to move any farther, I collapsed to the ground and put my back against a tree. Unlike the twisted trunks and branches near the castle I'd escaped from, these trees had almost green leaves, and a few had splashes of color from fruit or flowers.

I doubted I was safe, but forcing myself to move proved more than I could manage, and my eyelids fluttered shut against my will.

I startled awake sometime later from a quiet voice.

"There you are."

I jerked my head upright and gasped as it smacked into something hard. The tree I'd fallen asleep against. "Ow," I whined.

"This isn't a safe place to nap," the lightly accented voice chided.

The light had faded, and I had to squint, but finally I made out someone kneeling in front of me, just out of my reach.

No, it wasn't that dark. It was more that the being in front of me seemed to be made at least partially of the shadow stuff. At this point, it didn't even faze me.

"Who are you?"

"Nic," he answered quietly, "and you are Ember."

"Nic?" I scrambled to my knees and nearly did a face plant as my muscles seized up.

A hand shifted out of the swirl of shadow and steadied me.

"I'm supposed to find you."

The shadow retreated farther, revealing a man with startlingly familiar features. Baz hadn't sparked my memory, but Nic did. Shit. I knew him. From where, though? He had his longer dark hair tied back in a small tail, and if the lighting wasn't tricking me, he had tawny brown skin and deep-set angular brown eyes. High cheekbones accented a handsome face, and a darker shadow followed his jaw line—literal five o'clock shadow?

"And you have found me," he replied. The shadows swirled around him again, and I lost my fix on his features for a moment.

67

"We have to get out of here. Dear old Baz has noticed your absence, and I'm sure he's released the hounds."

I staggered to my feet, his hand still on my arm, solid though the rest of him seemed to be made of shadow.

"Hounds?" Moving stiffly, I took a few steps to loosen my muscles.

"We do not want to get caught by them, I promise."

Nic solidified again, now standing, though I hadn't seen the transition. He was tall, slender, and broad shouldered. He wore a long-sleeved t-shirt and dark jeans—I thought. No, it looked more like slacks now, and a button-down shirt. Wait…No, his clothes were definitely shifting, along with some of his features. It was as if his hair couldn't settle on a length, and occasionally parts of him simply dissolved into shadow, only to reform moments later.

Trippy…

"How are we going to outrun hounds?" I hated how scared my voice sounded, but damn it, I was terrified.

Nic glanced around before gesturing. A few shadows detached from trunks of trees or piles of rocks and scattered.

"They'll try to draw the hounds off, and we'll go as quickly as we can." Nic set off through the woods.

"I have so many questions." I hurried after as best as I was able.

"I imagine you do," he answered, his soft accent enjoyable and oh, so familiar. Kiwi? Was he from New Zealand? I remembered a few actors from that region that I enjoyed listening to.

"Are you going to answer them?"

"If we don't get killed escaping from Baz and his hounds, I'll do my best."

Taking the hint when Nic didn't elaborate, I remained quiet and concentrated on staying with him. He was hard to keep track of, at times difficult to make out amongst the swirling shadow stuff that was prevalent even here, and in other instances completely solid.

I trudged onward, vision narrowing to where I thought Nic was. Exhaustion made it hard to concentrate, and hunger gnawed at my stomach. We'd been walking long enough that my adrenalin had faded, and my feet dragged.

"Stop that," Nic snarled.

I lurched to a halt, inches from stepping into a murky pool of water. The swirl of lighter shadow I'd been following dissipated, laughter sounding around us.

Nic solidified next to me, putting a hand on my arm. "My apologies. I seem to have lost you to the will-o'wisp."

I nearly lost it, keeping back the sobs and the fear by sheer force of will.

"You look done in. I suppose I can imagine why."

Without asking, and before I could object, Nic swept me up into his arms and continued on at a much faster pace.

"You're just going to carry me, then?" Irritation warred with exhaustion and fear. It was inconclusive which feeling won the fight, but I thought it might have been the fatigue.

"Yes. For now. We can rest at the old cabin for a short time while I see if the shades drew off the hounds."

"What if they didn't?"

"Then we're in real trouble. All the mirrors are broken."

With those cryptic words, he fell silent, and I just didn't have the energy to ask any more questions.

Though Nic's features still shifted in and out of shadow, he remained mostly solid while he held me. The warmth from his body and his friendly presence nearly undid me again. I was not some weeping child, but I couldn't deny I was in distress, and boy did I need saving. While Nic wasn't my knight, right now I was grateful for any real help I could get. Geraint had told me to find Nic. I hoped he'd known what he was doing. Hell, I prayed he was still alive.

I rubbed at my nose and continued to fight off tears at the thought of my knight in the hands of cruel Prince Baz.

"Not much farther," Nic assured me.

I lost track of time, staring at the dark material of Nic's shirt and impressed that he didn't seem at all tired from having me in his arms.

"Could you get the door for me, luv?"

Jerking myself out of a daze, I twisted in Nic's arms and froze. *I know that cabin. How…?*

"You're not as light as you seem," he prompted.

"Sorry." I grabbed the knob and jiggled it before turning the handle.

Nic sucked in a breath in surprise. "You remember?"

"I guess so," I murmured.

"I wasn't sure you would remember anything. We were all so young."

It was as if his words, combined with the very familiar interior of the cabin, opened a floodgate of memories. Memories I couldn't believe I'd forgotten.

"Wait," I whispered. "How is this possible?"

Nic squeezed me gently in his arms before setting me on the ancient couch pushed up against one wall of the tiny one-room cabin. He dissolved almost completely into darkness, as if exhausted from the effort of remaining solid as long as he had. Nic reached out of the cloud of shadow and shut the door before partially reforming and sinking down into one of the surprisingly sturdy chairs at the old table. Four chairs. There had been four children playing at this cabin nearly every afternoon for several years.

The room also had an ancient iron stove I remembered using to pretend to heat our lunches with, and a mirror over a spot that might have held a bed at one time. The only difference from my twenty-some-odd-year-old memories were the cracks and fractures splitting the mirror, and I thought I remembered an ornate frame where this mirror had none.

This same cabin sat in the woods outside my parents' home. I'd played here as a kid for several years as soon as I'd been old enough to roam away from the immediate area around my house, but I hadn't visited it since, for whatever reason. I'd never even sketched it, though I'd drawn everything else.

"Nic, I don't understand."

He took a deep breath and nodded. "I'll do my best. You were eight, I believe, when we first met?"

"I think so."

He chuckled. "You were very insistent that you were eight, and that you were plenty old enough to play in the woods, if I remember correctly."

Smiling, my cheeks heated. "That sounds like me."

"My brothers and I had just discovered our first arch that wasn't heavily guarded." He gestured toward the mirror, "And we were keen to explore the waking world. Mary was kind enough to let us through." Nic grinned, looking at the floor as if lost in thought. "All three of us were terrified when you came crashing out of the woods toward us. At first, we thought you were some sort of monster with as much noise as you made. We weren't much reassured when we realized you were a human child."

"I think I remember coaxing you, and the other two out of the shadows. Dio, right? Dio loved tag." I grinned at the memory. "And Baz? I don't remember him being like this." That he hated me now was like a punch to the gut.

71

What had happened? "It didn't take long before we played almost every day, though."

"No, we were easily convinced to come out and play, and he wasn't."

"So, if that's an arch." I pointed to the mirror and made a guess. "Can't we use it to go home?"

Nic leaned back in his chair, crossing his arms, and staring at me. After a moment, he clenched his jaw and shrugged. "All the arches except the one in Nightmare Castle are broken."

I wrinkled my brow. "Nightmare Castle? Seriously, that's what it's called? That's like something out of an eighties cartoon."

He shook his head, amusement crinkling the skin at the corners of his eyes. "I believe that's what you said the first time we told you what our home was called."

"We need to rescue Geraint and we need to get home," I said as the reality of my current situation intruded on pleasant memories.

"Geraint?" Nic tilted his head.

"My partner. They took him when they took me."

"Ahh, your knight."

A chill crawled icy fingers down my spine. I hunched, holding my stomach. "He knows, doesn't he?"

"Your knight? We sent him to keep you safe. He's done his job."

"He's… he's my friend."

"Good. It would have been much more difficult to stay close to you if he hadn't become your friend."

Nic seemed to think that was it, but despite the complicated emotions bouncing around in my chest, I wasn't giving up on the idea of rescuing Geraint.

"We need to rescue him. If they didn't kill him after I escaped."

Nic frowned, but dozens of creepy voices echoing around the cabin cut off whatever reply he intended.

"Nic," the female voice repeated.

I whimpered, but Nic stood and hurried to the mirror. "Mary?"

When Nic didn't seem alarmed at the voice despite his tense shoulders and narrowed eyes, I forced myself to my feet and went to his side. The shattered mirror showed dozens of the same terrifying visage that had opened the arch for us back on Earth ages ago.

"They come," dozens of her said from the mirror, giving her voice a creepy echo.

He spun around, looking toward the door.

"You cannot get caught," she continued. "Nic, you must leave the princess and flee."

I clutched my arms and rocked on my heels. I couldn't go back. "Can't the mirror be fixed?"

Nic turned back and studied me before glancing at the dozens of Marys in the mirror.

"I do not have the power to fix the mirror," he said. "You're welcome to try."

"Me?"

"You are the Princess of Nightmare. It's possible you can repair the arch where I cannot."

"But—"

"You must escape, Nic," the Marys said again.

"I'm not leaving Ember."

"You know, I don't remember Baz being such a douche canoe. Hell, I recognized you almost immediately, and I still can't imagine any connection between present day Baz and the kid I used to play with. Where's Dio?" My thoughts strayed to my third playmate.

"We don't know, and no, Baz wasn't like this until about ten years ago."

"You are surrounded," the Marys hissed.

"Fix the mirror, Princess," Nic ordered.

"We're going to talk about this Princess thing," I muttered as I studied the shattered glass, trying to ignore the terrifying woman staring back at me. I'd been able to command the shadow. Maybe this was the same thing?

"Is it okay if I touch it?" I asked Mary.

She nodded and retreated deeper into the mirror, disappearing from the smaller fragments, and looking quite distant in the pieces she still appeared in.

How a flat piece of glass with silver backing could have depth, I didn't know, but I'd already walked through one of these things, so really, I wasn't going to question anything right now.

Hounds bayed in the distance, and chills goose-bumped my skin.

"Fuck," I muttered, and put my trembling hand against the cold glass.

"Hurry," Nic said with little conviction. He clearly didn't think I could fix it.

The baying hounds closed in on our location. Their cries grated against my nerves, like nails raking a chalkboard.

Well, screw him. I was going to repair this damn arch, and I was going to go home. As I'd done with the shadow stuff, I visualized the mirror in one piece.

The fabric that covered my body slid along my arm and coated the mirror. Not exactly sure that was what I was going for, I tried to call the shadow stuff back to me, especially since the fabric had retreated from my legs, leaving me shivering, though still technically clothed.

The door burst inward.

Glancing over my shoulder, I saw Nic take one of the hound's heads off with a sword, blade gleaming dully in the not-light of this world. The hound disintegrated into shadow stuff, but two more pushed through the door, eyes glowing red, coats a dull black, teeth bared and ready to rip through me and Nic.

"Hurry, Princess," the Marys urged.

I turned my back on the fight and focused on repairing the cracks in the mirror. That actually wasn't difficult. The glass flowed under my hand until only a single terrifying woman stared back at me from the depths of the mirror.

"I fixed it," I shouted.

Nic looked back. One hound took advantage and leaped at him. Nic melted into shadow and the hound tumbled to the ground. It scrambled to its feet, red eyes focused on me, but Nic reformed behind it, beheading the hound with his sword before it could tear me limb from limb.

I hadn't even realized I was moaning in terror until the creature was gone.

Nic came to my side, sword vanishing into the shadowy mist.

"Mary?"

"The mirror is fixed. The arch is still broken."

"What?" I yelped.

Nic put his back to mine as more hounds crowded into the single room, growls filling the space. I should have been able to smell their breath, feel the heat from their panting exhalations, but while the scrape of their paws on the wooden floor and their threatening growls were very real, they seemed to be all sound and shadow, no actual substance.

Until one slammed into Nic. He hit my back with his as he scrambled to keep the creature from tearing his throat out. Tendrils of black snaked off the walls and grabbed the hounds, throwing them backward.

"Fix it, Ember, or we're both dead," Nic snarled at me.

Screaming, I put both hands against the glass, shoving my will and the shadow stuff I wore into the mirror, picturing the arch I'd seen when I was kidnapped and thinking only of escaping to my home.

After a second that stretched into eternity, something clicked like a key opening a lock, and I fell into the mirror, dragging Nic with me.

CHAPTER 6

Ember

Memories

"One, two, three..."

I ran through the woods while Nic counted. He always found me, so I needed to find a great hiding place this time. He usually discovered the others, too, before they got back to base, but he always got me, and it sucked.

Pushing my bottom lip out as I thought, I came up with a plan. It was a bad idea, but I really didn't want to get caught every time. We weren't supposed to go anywhere near the caves without an adult, but as long as they didn't find out, it would be fine. And it wasn't like I was going to go very far in. Just enough to get out of sight.

Dried leaf litter cracked under my feet and a twig snapped, but Nic was still counting to a hundred loud enough to cover my noise as I crashed through the woods. Dio and Baz would find good places to hide, too, but I knew these woods better than any of them. Which made it even more frustrating that Nic always found where I hid.

Panting as I raced toward the caves, I cast around for the faint trail my family had made. We came out here a couple of times a year and explored, but not often enough to make it easy to find. I loved the area. We usually found cool rocks and stuff for the rock garden back at the house.

A waterfall and a pool of water I also wasn't supposed to go into without an adult around made this area the best on really hot days. It wasn't warm enough today to go behind the waterfall and if I came home soaked, they'd know I wasn't following the rules.

I always followed the rules. My playtime with my forest friends was too important, but maybe just this once...

Stopping near a pile of gray boulders, I put my hand on the cool stone and caught my breath. As soon as my harsh pants quieted, I listened. I couldn't hear Nic anymore. He'd probably gotten to a hundred. Not wanting to get caught out in the open, I crouched and scurried toward the cave entrance. The caves we normally explored had a wide opening, but the one I headed for had a kid-sized crack to squeeze through. After a quick hesitation, I plunged into the small space, scrambled over some rock piles, and crouched down behind the boulders that would shield me from view. See, I am barely in the cave at all.

Settling in to wait, I put my back against the rock, wiped sweat from my brow, and tried to quiet my breathing so I wouldn't give myself away. No way would Nic find me in here.

Sure enough, the minutes stretched. I glanced at my pink kitty watch, but not enough time had passed for me to be "safe."

A cool breeze from farther in the cave cooled my sweat-soaked skin, and I shivered. There must be an entrance higher up. I shifted as carefully as I could to avoid making any noise. I thought I heard boys laughing. Maybe Nic had found Dio or Baz?

As the minutes stretched, scary stories we told each other intruded on my thoughts, and my skin crawled. I both did and didn't want to look deeper into the cave. Unfortunately, I was listening so intently that other sounds reached me. *Is that a clatter of rocks? What would make the rocks move?*

I shifted again and glanced at my watch, moving my arm into a shaft of light so I could see the time. Darn, still not enough time to be safe, although I was approaching a record. Nic had usually found me by now.

This time I did hear rocks sliding. I stifled a yelp and stared into the darkness. *Was that breathing? A quiet growl? Why had I come here?*

Wishing for a flashlight, I forced myself to peer into the darkness. I could see a little way into the cave, but a sharp bend kept most of it from view. Anything could be lurking around that corner. Bears... big cats... monsters... Okay, probably not bears. I could barely wriggle through that space. Bats... Maybe it was bats? I'd be okay if it were bats because they wouldn't come out during the day.

But what if it was a monster?

I whimpered and glanced frantically at my kitty watch. Almost time. So close. I could hide a little longer. If I didn't make any noise, whatever it was, wouldn't know I was here? Right?

There was definitely something back there, but I'd been hiding for twenty minutes now. I was safe from Nic, but whatever was staring at me might come get me at any minute. I scrambled out of my hiding place, the loose rocks sliding under my feet. Normally, that wouldn't have been an issue, but I was in such a hurry to run away from the monster in the dark that I didn't pay attention to my feet and slipped. The rocks shifted, and my foot plunged into a small crevasse while another rock rolled on top, trapping me.

Panic tightened my throat and my heart pounded in my chest. Any minute now, the monster in the dark might get me.

The boys yelled my name in the distance. Something scraped on the rocks behind me.

I screamed.

CHAPTER 7

Ember

This time, instead of a relatively smooth transition through the mirror where I walked—or was dragged—from one side to the other, we tumbled uncontrolled through the arch, with a slight resistance at the end. It was almost as if whatever magic allowed us to move between mirrors didn't want to let me go through to the other side. There was no way I was going back, however, so I shoved my will at the resistance, and we tumbled through.

And kept dropping.

I shrieked.

Something grabbed me at the last minute, slowing my fall and cushioning me so the ground didn't hurt nearly as much as it would have. I was lucky, too, because even cushioned, my head came down on something hard with a sharp corner.

"Ember!" someone shouted.

I clamped my mouth shut on the screams.

"Ember, are you all right?" That was Nic. Who else had spoken?

Forcing my eyes open, I quickly took in my surroundings.

Home. We'd come out through the big mirror over the fireplace, and I probably had Nic to thank for not cracking my head open on the stonework. My parents and my cousin Ash stared at us incredulously.

I scrambled to my feet. Or tried to. The room tilted and Nic crouched next to me, grabbing my arms.

"Ember?" My dad reached for me.

Ash came forward and threw a blanket over my shoulders.

"Who the hell are you?" Ash glared at Nic.

"And how did you come out of the mirror?" my mom added, voice shaky.

"And where is Geraint?" Dad asked, and between the three of them, they'd pretty much covered all the relevant questions.

"All of that, and why are you naked?" Ash finished.

I glanced down at myself. "I was totally wearing clothing on the other side of the mirror," I protested.

"You used the dream essence to repair the arch," Nic explained quietly.

"Oh. Sure. Of course, I did." I wrapped the blanket around myself and sagged back to the ground. Nic put his hand on my shoulder to steady me.

I both wanted to shrug him off and to crawl into his arms and cry. I did note that he was a lot more solid on this side of the mirror.

"Ember? Are you okay?" Ash prompted.

"Uh. No. Not really. Why are you here?"

"You and Knight have been missing for a week." She crouched down in front of me.

"Shit. Robby! Is Robby okay?"

"He's fine. Someone gave him a concussion, and he doesn't remember much, but he's okay," Ash supplied.

I took a deep breath. "Okay. Good. I really don't know how to answer your other questions."

"Perhaps you should get cleaned up, get some food, and then we can talk." Nic's voice flattened at the last bit, and I guessed he was not at all happy to have the audience.

"Who are you again?" Ash shifted her attention from me to the shadow prince.

"Nic," he replied sharply.

"He's fine, Ash. And Nic's right. Help me up?" I said to Nic.

Gently, he supported me while I got to my feet. I took a minute to lean against him and get my balance before stepping away.

"But you came through a mirror!" my mom protested.

"Yeah, it's a whole thing," I snapped, unable to deal with anything else.

"Let's let Ember get cleaned up," Ash soothed. "We'll get answers in a minute. At least she's safe, and I'm sure she's hungry."

My parents backed off, but their wide-eyed stares never left me or Nic.

"Okay, why don't you hang out here, and I'll be back," I said to the prince.

Nic glanced up at the mirror, then back at me, smiling wryly and a touch unhappily. "For now, at least, I'm stuck here."

I followed his gaze. The mirror had shattered in its frame.

"Shit," I muttered.

"Mary might have cracked it for us," he supplied. "Breaking the trail and all that."

My parents and Ash stared at us, but didn't throw any more demands for answers our way.

"Food sounds amazing," I said, latching onto that subject. I let Ash put her arm around me and lead me from our cozy den. My parents headed for the kitchen, looking a little dazed.

"I recognize him," Ash blurted as soon as we were alone. "He looks like an older version of one of those boys you used to draw."

I'd drawn so many things over the years. I'd forgotten about that, too. Not Ash, though. She was sharp as a tack and her memory had to be near perfect. It made her a fantastic lawyer.

"Yeah. About that," I said, but didn't know how to continue.

"Okay, let's get you cleaned up first. I'll stop pestering you."

It was a hundred percent obvious she couldn't wait to hear my story. I didn't blame her, though. I mean, we'd come crashing out of a mirror.

"Okay, one last question, and then I'll stop. Is Geraint okay?" Ash almost never called him anything but Knight, and it caught me off guard when she used his first name.

"No. I don't know. Maybe?" I rubbed at my eyes, smearing the remains of my stage makeup.

"Shit, Ember. What happened?"

I sighed. Clearly, I wasn't getting to put this off. "Just let me wash my face."

"Yeah. Sorry."

Ash followed me into the bedroom I shared with Geraint. The familiar space filled with touches of me and Geraint nearly brought me to my knees.

Pictures I'd drawn covered the walls. Some were framed, but most just sketches of landscapes that Geraint had hung with sticky tack. I'd taken some time with the one I'd done of the two of us. It was a drawing of a selfie we'd taken in Mexico. We'd been sightseeing between shows on a six-month contract down there. I'd snapped the selfie just before he'd kissed me for the first time. Like, really kissed me, not just a friendly peck on the cheek or forehead, like we'd exchanged for years.

84

"Ember, is he hurt?"

"Ash, I really don't know. Let me wash my face."

I dropped the blanket from my shoulders, leaving it on the ground. Ash picked it up and put it on the rocking chair in the corner where Geraint often sat reading while I drew at my desk.

Geraint and I had an attached bathroom, and I went in there and stared in the mirror. Grays and blacks smeared my skin, as if I'd taken charcoal and ash and rubbed it all over my face. I knew I'd been using color when I'd applied the makeup, but it was made of shadow stuff. Essence? Is that what Nic had said? Dream essence.

My normally bouncy hair was flat and tangled. If I were still in Nightmare, I'd probably have sticks and leaves in it. Scratches covered my arms and a few lines in my smeared makeup made me think I would have scratches there, too.

My wrist ached where I'd run into the tree, and other injuries were making themselves known. The *fun* game Baz had created, dropping me and catching me, had bruised me up pretty badly, and the marks stood out on my otherwise tan skin. I was sure Ash had noticed.

I was used to having some bruises, especially when I pulled out my lyra since the metal hoop wasn't kind to skin, but I looked like I'd been beaten.

Peering deeply into the mirror, I searched for any traces of nightmare, or Mary, or arches, or anything. All I saw was my smeared face, Ash leaning against the doorframe, and the rest of the bathroom. Somewhat reassured that we were alone, I focused on cleaning up.

I pulled out some makeup remover and hoped it was still good. I hadn't been in this room since last summer. Traces of the leather and cedar soap Geraint used mingled with the eucalyptus I loved. His comb he'd forgotten at the beginning of our travels last fall lay on the counter next to some shaving cream, just waiting for us to return.

"Damn it," I muttered and angrily turned the faucet.

Ash came in and turned on the shower so it could warm and checked to make sure I still had soap.

Shooting her a grateful look, I tested the water and got in.

"Okay, so, this is going to sound insane," I started.

"Spark, you came out of a mirror." She had actually been the first one to use that nickname.

"Okay. Point." I launched into the tale of what had happened while I showered. I nearly used Geraint's soap, but at the last second went for the body wash we shared instead.

When I was done with my tale, I stepped out of the shower. Ash handed me a towel and retreated to give me space to dry off. She threw comfortable clothing at me when I left the bathroom. Numbly, I dressed in the sweats and a loose top, and waited for her reaction.

When she didn't say anything, I glanced at her. She had her brown hair cut short to pass for professional in her everyday life, but with a little gel could become extraordinary and punk. Right now, she wore a racerback tank top and jeans, which showed off the fantastically colorful full sleeves she had on both her arms. The circus themed tattoo she, Geraint, and I had all gotten was just visible on her shoulder when she turned her back to me. You'd never know she had all that ink in her professional clothing, but this was her natural state.

While she didn't perform much anymore, she was a talented lyra aerialist and when we'd been younger, we'd had a few killer doubles routines. She still practiced every day, and her muscles were every bit as impressive as my own.

"Ash?"

"If you hadn't come out of a mirror, I wouldn't believe any of this," she said with a small laugh and a shake of her head. "Okay, so you just spent the last week in Nightmare?"

"Yeah. I really don't know how much time it was for me, but a week feels about right."

"And Geraint is still trapped there?"

"Yeah. He somehow helped me escape."

"And Nic is one of your imaginary friends from when you were like eight, right?"

"Uh, yeah. I guess so."

"Not so imaginary?"

I snorted. "He's a prince of Nightmare. I'm not sure if that makes him extra imaginary or what."

She smiled at that. "And you're a princess?"

"No, but they keep calling me that."

Ash came over and put her arms around me. "Are you okay?"

"Physically? I'm banged up, but nothing I won't recover from."

"Okay, fair enough," she said when I didn't continue. "Let's go talk to your prince and see if we can figure out how to get him home and rescue Geraint. I'm sure he's just as freaked out as you are."

I took a deep breath and shook my head. "Ash, I think he knew."

"Wait, what?"

"Geraint. I think he knew about Dream being an actual place, and, uh, the rest."

Ash squeezed me. "Well, we still need to rescue him."

"Yeah, we do." I collapsed my shoulders and hugged myself. At least I'd proven one thing wrong. I wasn't trapped in Nightmare. I wasn't dreambound like Baz had said I would be. That was something. Right?

***

Ash and I left my bedroom and headed toward the kitchen. Our house was an old, but large, log cabin. Mine and Geraint's room was on the main level, not too far from the den. My parents had their room on the upper floor on the far side of the house. It gave us all some privacy when I was home. We had a handful of guest rooms that occasionally got used, a library, a more public living room, and a kitchen sufficient to feed an army.

The rest of the property had cabins for the summer camp, our gym, both indoor and outdoor, gardens everywhere, a host of chickens and other fowl, and a couple of livestock guardian dogs to help keep the birds safe.

Surrounding that were the woods I'd played in constantly, and beyond that the true wilderness, the hills, and mountains of the Allegheny range.

The wooden floor creaked as we walked, a familiar, comforting sound. The smell of food cooking was incredibly obvious after a week of next to nothing but the dry dusty scents of Nightmare. Even the food I'd eaten hadn't smelled as strongly as good home cooking. From the garlic and tomato aroma, I guessed mom was making the ultimate comfort food. Spaghetti with homemade sauce. Dad cooked the sauce in huge batches, and they froze enough to get through several months at a time. Mom occasionally made homemade noodles, but today they'd probably be out of a box, unless she'd already had some on hand.

They had modernized the kitchen when they'd started doing summer camps. That had been years ago, but the large range top with gas burners, huge refrigerator and freezer, and industrial-sized dishwasher were all stainless. The counter tops were all granite, and they designed several as easily cleanable cutting surfaces. Pots and pans hung from a rack in the ceiling. Over the summer, they had a professional cooking team, and everyone ate on the screened porch on the other side of the house. We kept part of the house private, but the living room, kitchen and porches were fair game for all the people who stayed with us.

Memories filled me with some sense of calm, grounding me in the present. I was home. I was safe.

Mom was heating something over the stove and boiling water. I was right, comfort food for the win. Dad stared at Nic. For his part, Nic had sought out the deepest shadow he could find and was standing in it. Come to think of it, I'd rarely seen him out in full sunlight even when we were kids.

Ash pulled my normal seat out at the table and gestured for me to sit. Grateful, I sank into the chair, groaning.

"Okay, so first off, who beat you and how do we destroy that fucker?" Ash sat next to me, arms crossed, looking murderous.

Nic frowned, coming partially out of the shadow he hid in. "Someone beat you?"

"Not exactly." I shied away from the memories of falling. "Uh." I didn't want to talk about it, or even say his name. Now that I had remembered my childhood friends, I couldn't believe Baz had changed so much.

"Let me guess, the douche canoe was inventively unkind," Nic supplied.

I snorted. "That's one way to put it. Yeah, no one touched me."

"Clearly, he didn't have to," Nic growled.

I shrugged. "The silks did most of the damage. He made me fall a bunch."

Nic's expression turned murderous, matching Ash's.

"Does the douche canoe have a name?" Dad asked, and I realized I hadn't told them the same thing I'd told Ash.

"Uh, did Nic fill you in on anything?"

"No, your friend has been quite silent about everything." Dad tightened his jaw.

Taking a deep breath and shooting Nic an annoyed look, I again launched into the story I'd told Ash.

By the time I had finished, my parents were wide-eyed and Nic looked even unhappier. Had he not expected me to tell my parents everything? Well, I'd left out some details, like the princess part.

"Why would these nightmare beings want to kidnap you?" Mom finally asked.

"I don't know," I replied.

Unfortunately, that just meant that Dad turned their question to Nic.

The prince narrowed his eyes at me before stepping out of the shadows completely. I kicked out a chair so he could join us at the table. After a considering glance at my parents, he accepted.

When Nic stepped out of the shadows, the strange shifting nature of some of his features solidified into long hair tied back in a tail, black slacks, and a black short sleeved button-down shirt. I wasn't even sure if that was what he'd been wearing the last time I looked at him when we'd first arrived. His tawny skin appeared a little wan, and he had shadows under his deep-set angular eyes. The stubble along his jaw was more pronounced, though it only accented his handsome features.

"Prince Baz, the douche canoe, wants her because he thinks she's the princess Nightmare needs to stop the spread of the nothingness that is overtaking Dream."

"That doesn't sound good," Ash said. "I'm assuming Dream is literally connected to human dreams?"

Nic inclined his head in agreement.

"So if Dream gets overtaken with nothing, what replaces it?" Ash continued.

"Nothing, so far as we can tell," Nic replied.

"Well, that's a whole lot of bad for everyone. Humans can't survive without dreams." Ash cut to the heart of that problem quickly.

"No, and obviously none of us wish to cease to exist. I sincerely doubt Baz has Nightmare's best interests at heart, however."

"Some of the girls in his weird circus collection said they thought he wanted to sacrifice the princess to the nothingness to get it to go away," I said.

"That's a bizarre theory." Nic's brow furrowed as he thought.

Something else occurred to me. Geraint had told me to make sure Nic knew Baz hadn't recognized me. I wasn't sure if I wanted to go into it more in front of my parents, however. Ash, yes. My parents... maybe not.

Nic glanced at me, as if catching that I'd had a thought.

I gave him a quick shake of my head.

"But she's not, right?" Mom said a little too quickly. "We have plenty of unbroken mirrors to send you home with, and she can stay here, safe."

"There is much we still need to discover," Nic replied in a nice non-answer.

"Whatever else is going on, we have to rescue Geraint before I can be nice and safe anywhere," I said.

Nic clenched his jaw, but didn't object in front of my parents.

"Okay, food," Ash declared. "We're not going to figure out anything on an empty stomach. Nic, do you eat human food, or do you, like, drink blood or something?"

He raised his eyebrows. "I am not a vampire. I can eat human food."

"Wait, vampires are real?" Ash leaned forward. She might have a tiny obsession. I hid a smirk behind my hand.

"As real as anything from Dream is real." Nic was good at those non-answers.

"We're going to revisit this," she replied before getting up and grabbing plates. "Ember, I texted Robby. He's on his way with your equipment. We haven't notified the cops yet because I imagine you probably need to figure out something to tell them that they'll believe."

"Great." I didn't even want to think about dealing with the cops.

"So, let's eat. Then I want to show you the new setup in the gym. You'll love it." She carried on while we all served ourselves, keeping us from awkward silence or even more awkward questions. I really loved my cousin, now more than ever. She'd always been my favorite.

Food helped a ton. Nic even appeared to enjoy the meal, and he'd mostly answered the few questions my parents were brave enough to ask. I was sure he knew Ash and I were going to drill him later, but at least right now he acted mostly at ease.

My parents took care of cleaning up, shooing us out of the kitchen after a significant look at Ash. Yeah, they wanted her to get all the information we weren't telling them. Fortunately, I trusted her to be cautious about what she shared. They were taking this remarkably well, come to think of it.

Nic followed me and my cousin out of the kitchen and to the back door. Daylight lingered and the heat and humidity shimmered in the air. It wasn't even fully summer, but today had obviously been warm. Birds sang and the riot of colors from the spring flowers filled my heart to bursting. Especially after the grays and blacks of Nightmare.

Speaking of Nightmare, Nic hadn't followed us outside. He lingered just inside the door, out of the direct sunlight.

I turned and went back to the house. "No sunlight?" I asked him.

"I can do sunlight. It's simply draining and very uncomfortable. Where are we headed?"

I pointed to the extensive building off to the west. We had to go through the gardens and across an open grassy area we kept mowed and used for outdoor practice.

Nic took a breath and nodded, then followed me into the sunlight. In the shade, his skin tone was either the blacks and grays of shadows or tawny brown. The sunlight grayed his skin unhealthily.

"You're not joking about the sun."

"I'll survive." He even sounded less vibrant.

Though I wanted to admire the garden, I lengthened my stride for Nic's sake.

"So, Nic, what are you, then?" Ash questioned the prince.

"I'm a prince of Nightmare," he replied, as if that answered everything.

"Yeah, but what does that mean?"

"It means I'm one of three charged with keeping some semblance of order in the realm of Nightmare. Mostly that involves making sure especially powerful nightmares don't bleed over into the conscious realm. Though we've neglected that duty as of late."

"Who are the other two?"

"Baz and Dio. We haven't seen Dio in years, and Baz has changed significantly."

Ash unlocked the door when we reached the gym, and let us inside. We only kept it locked when unoccupied by an adult to make sure none of the campers used the equipment alone. We didn't want anyone to get hurt.

Nic took a relieved breath once we were out of the sun. The building was nice and cool, and dark.

Ash hesitated with her hand over the light switch. "We'll just leave them off for a minute."

"Thank you," Nic replied from the shadows. I couldn't even see him when I turned to look.

"So, Nic, Baz, Dio, your parents have a thing for three letter names?"

"Did yours?" Nic shot back.

"Touché," Ash replied. "No, I picked this name to match Ember's. She's always been one of my best friends, and when I transitioned, I wanted something that went with hers."

"Ahh. I like it." Nic stepped out of the shadow and put his hand over the light switch. "I'm recovered if you would prefer lights."

"Unlike you, shadow boy, we can't see in the dark," Ash replied.

He flipped on the lights, wincing a little but otherwise seeming unaffected by the artificial illumination.

"To answer your question, Nic is short for Nyctophobia. I'm the embodiment of the fear of the dark or the unknown."

"So, the fear of the dark has a Kiwi accent?" She grinned at Nic.

He shrugged. "In this lifetime I do."

"Okay, Nic, why are you not excited about the idea of helping me rescue Geraint? Because I don't know if I can do it without you, and I need him back." I twisted my hands together. There was so much we needed to figure out, but this was the most important. At least to me.

"His job was to keep you safe. He's essentially fulfilled that duty. You're safe. As soon as we find an appropriate mirror, I can try to sneak back into Nightmare, and hopefully, you can avoid further notice." Nic was studying the gym equipment and didn't see the color drain from my face when he confirmed what I'd suspected.

"What do you mean?" Ash demanded.

"The one you call Geraint is a knight, created from dream essence to fulfill a purpose. In this case, protecting our princess." Nic turned just in time to grab my arm and keep me on my feet as my world tilted.

"But he's real," I blurted, sagging in Nic's grasp.

"And what do you mean, princess?" Ash demanded.

"The knight is real enough," Nic allowed. "And Ember is Nightmare's princess, and you may be the key to stopping this nothingness, but I find that highly unlikely. Therefore, there is no need for you to return to a place you have no wish to be, and there is no need for you to trouble yourself about the knight."

"Geraint is my best friend. Well, him and Ash. I'm not going to just walk away from him, even if he is some sort of nightmare person." I stomped my foot. "And what the hell do you mean I'm the princess? That's not even possible."

Nic released my arm and twisted away, momentarily dissolving into shadow before reforming a few feet away.

"We were children. We'd found an unguarded mirror, and Mary let us through. I told you this. The four of us played as often as we could, as your world was safer and much more entertaining. Do you recall one day when you got back from a vacation to see one of your relatives married?"

"Yeah, I think I do." Chills traveled down my spine, and my hands trembled. I thought I knew where he was going with this.

"Well, it turns out when a human child plays at having a wedding with the child princes of Nightmare, it's binding," he continued bitterly.

"I take it you didn't know?"

"No, of course not," he snapped. "None of us did until a couple of years later."

"Oh." I twisted my hands together and stared at the floor. "I'm sorry."

"It's not anyone's fault," Ash said. "I take it you found out the hard way?"

"You could say that." Nic didn't elaborate. "Still, the knight was created to keep you safe after our mistake was discovered. We were also forbidden from using the arches. Which is why we vanished from your life."

I sighed. "This is a lot."

Ash put her arms around me, and I leaned against her. "So, what do we do?"

"I told you. We find a mirror, and get Mary to sneak me back into Nightmare. I'll make it seem like you were killed when escaping, and hopefully, Baz will turn his attention elsewhere."

"Nic, we have to rescue Geraint."

The prince took a deep breath. "Why?"

"He's my partner. I need him." I didn't even try to hide the desperation I felt at the thought of losing Geraint.

Nic's expression darkened. "Oh, really…"

Ash crossed her arms. "It's not like the three of you were here. It wasn't like Geraint just jumped into her bed. He didn't even agree until she started looking for the next best option. So, chill the fuck out. Also, which one of you did she pretend to marry, anyway?"

"All three of them," I answered with a groan.

"Well, Nic here clearly isn't happy about it. So, why are you suddenly feeling possessive?"

Nic took a deep breath, then another, as if trying to not lose his temper. "The other issue with rescuing your knight is that there is only one unbroken arch in all of Nightmare, and that is the one in Nightmare Castle, where Baz currently has control of everything. He may not kill me if he catches me, but it won't be pleasant. He's so far ignored the beings under my care, focusing his games and entertainments on those more closely under his sway. If he figures out I'm involved with any of this that could change."

"Aren't you all three princes?" Ash pointed out.

"Yes, and somehow Baz seized all the power. It's complicated and not worth going into. The short answer is, I can likely get back and sneak through the shadows without getting caught. I very much doubt I'll be able to bring you with me, unless you wish to risk returning to Baz's tender care." Nic sounded even angrier, eyes narrowed, jaw clenched when he wasn't spitting words at me.

I blanched, hugging myself at that thought.

"No? Didn't think so."

"Then take me," Ash said. "We'll rescue Knight, you can sneak away, and he and I will come home. Then we don't risk Baz getting his hands on Ember."

"You can't come," Nic said. "You'd become dreambound, never able to leave Dream again. Only dreams can move between the conscious realm and the dream realm. Ember is a fortunate exception, because she *is* Nightmare's princess. That she could escape proves it."

Ash pursed her lips. "And you're not going to help Ember?"

"No."

"If she can go back and forth on her own, then she'll just have to do it without your help."

I wanted to protest, but I had come to the same conclusion that Ash had, and there was no way I was leaving Geraint behind if I could help it.

Nic shook his head. "I'll instruct Mary that you are not allowed access. If the opportunity arises to rescue your knight, I will, but it may be many years before it happens."

"Screw you, Nic," I gasped out, heart breaking all over again. "If I'm a princess, then she has to do what I say. I'm rescuing my knight and you're not going to stop me."

He smirked. "I think you'll find it's much more difficult than just declaring that you're the princess and forcing your way back into Nightmare to rescue your knight."

I flipped him off and turned my back. "Just leave. Find a fucking mirror and go through it and fucking leave."

"As you wish, your highness," Nic snapped and stalked out of the gym.

"Wow," Ash said once he was gone.

"Yeah," I agreed. "Can you just give me some time alone? Go make sure Nic finds his way out of here, please. I need a minute to process all this."

"Okay, Spark." Ash wrapped me in a tight hug, then left me alone in the gym.

Numbly, I began one of my stretching routines. I needed to get in the air and clear my head.

CHAPTER 8

Nic

Memories

Ember was supposed to be home today. The week she had been gone for a family gathering had seemed like an eternity. We didn't have the ability to visit her in her dreams yet, so we had to wait until we could see her in person.

Dio popped out from behind the rock he'd hidden behind and chased after Baz. I continued to bounce from shadow to shadow, heading for the cabin with the unguarded arch. Mary liked us. Mary would let us through. The other mirror dwellers weren't nearly as willing to convey three little princes with thin stories claiming they were granted permission.

My brothers generally made progress toward the forgotten cabin, so I didn't tell them to hurry. We were all eager to see Ember again. She was so much more colorful and interesting than anything in Nightmare.

We weren't supposed to wander far from the castle, either. Even though we were the princes, the right type of nightmare would eat us if they caught us.

Someday we'd be the scariest nightmares and would be able to go anywhere, but until then, we had to stick close to the castle.

Except we'd found the cabin and the arch.

Finally, we made it to the small building forgotten in the forest. Baz pushed open the door, and Dio and I followed him inside. I went straight to the mirror. Dio shoved his shoulder into mine, jostling me. Baz pushed in between us and then we all stood in front of the shiny surface.

"Bloody Mary," we intoned together, repeating the name three times.

The air chilled as Mary answered our call, surfacing in the mirror and grinning. "Young Princes," she said. Her voice was gentle, for all her appearance was grisly. I liked her glowing green eyes, though. Anything with a little color always caught my interest.

"Mary!" Dio exclaimed. "We're happy to see you. Can you take us to the cabin in the woods?"

"Little Prince, you are already in a cabin in the woods," Mary chided.

"Silly Mary," Baz said. "The one in the conscious realm that matches this cabin."

"Oh, that cabin," she teased.

"Please," I added.

"Of course, young princes. It is my honor to serve you." She stepped back, and the arch appeared.

Dio went first, I followed, and Baz came last, stepping into the cool mirror and following the path to the conscious realm.

The light was brighter than I preferred, but it always was in the conscious realm. I'd tolerate it for playtime with Ember.

We left the cabin and didn't have to wait long before our friend was crashing through the woods to meet us at our normal time.

"Boys!" she exclaimed. "I have a new game for us to play. I learned it while I was away."

"Does it involve jumping off trees into the water?" Baz asked.

"No, silly." She laughed. The sound was so pure and joyful it brought a smile to my lips.

"How about an extra special game of tag?" Dio offered.

"No. Not that, either." She glanced at me, waiting for my guess.

"It's not a new version of hide and seek?" I played her game, though I knew it would be something different.

"No, we're going to have a wedding." She spun in a circle, delighted with her idea. "First, we gotta get a whole bunch of flowers."

CHAPTER 9

Ember

"**E**mber?"

I whimpered, unable to even unlock my jaw enough to ask for help. I wasn't even sure what Ash could do to help me. Clutching the silks in a death grip, unable to release my foot locks where the fabric twisted around my feet and ankles, holding me in the sky. Unable to get down, I was frozen, and had been for at least twenty minutes.

She could have climbed up if I could unlock my foot from the silk and give her one to climb, but I was stuck in both, weight on one foot, the other leg wrapped to give me a seat. I clutched the fabric in front of me and couldn't let go. I'd thought working through my favorite solo routine would be a good way to think. I'd been wrong.

"Shit, what's wrong with her? She's never had a problem with heights."

"Likely a reaction to Baz's games. If you turn the lights off, I can get her down," Nic offered.

Why is he still here?

"How?"

"I'll use the shadows. Just turn the lights off, unless you have a better way?"

We had a rolling platform we used for rigging and stuff. Maybe they could get that—if I'd be able to make it down.

The lights went out, and I squeaked out another muffled cry.

"Ember." Nic's gently accented voice soothed me, containing none of the anger from earlier.

How did he get up here?

Arms wrapped around me, holding me tight.

"I promise I will never let you fall," he said. "Let go and hold on to me."

Tears leaked out from the corners of my eyes. I'd fallen and fallen and fallen, and I never wanted to fall again.

He gently pried my fingers off the silk, all the while murmuring to me how he'd never let me go.

My entire body shook as he slowly untangled me from my perch and pulled me into his arms. I buried my face against his chest and gripped his shirt hard enough to tear fabric—if he hadn't had some sort of weird dream material making up his clothing. Once he had my feet free, I wrapped my legs around his waist and clung to him like a monkey.

"You're lucky my body is relatively mutable," he grunted, "or you'd be crushing my ribs right now."

"Maybe you're lucky," I stammered.

He chuckled, and then we were sitting on the ground. I hadn't felt the transition at all. The lights flicked on, but I couldn't get my arms to relax. Terror still had me in its grip, though I was no longer in the air.

Terror of falling, but also fear that I might have lost my ability to fly. I lived for my time in the silks and in the straps. What if I could never go back? What if Baz had taken that from me, too?

"It's okay, Ember," Nic whispered, resting his cheek against my head. He held me tightly in his arms. "Take your time."

I sniffed, trying to hold back the tears, but his soft words broke the dam I'd built in the handful of hours I'd been home, and everything I'd been holding back burst forth. I sobbed in his arms, distantly aware that Ash had wrapped herself around me from the back.

It was probably only a few minutes, but I felt like I'd cried for hours by the time the flood of tears stopped.

"Sorry," I choked out.

"We all gotta ugly cry sometimes, Spark," Ash said.

Nic tightened his arms around me briefly.

"Thought you were leaving," I said, still speaking against his chest.

"It turns out we broke the only suitable mirror," he said.

"You can't use just any mirror?" The question pulled me out of some of my funk.

"Only mirrors backed with silver."

"What about the cabin mirror?"

"It's broken as well." Something about the way Nic held me made me feel like he was happy to have me there, despite his anger earlier. He held me the way Geraint did, possessively, as if he wouldn't let anything bad happen to me if he could help it.

I wanted to sink into that feeling and pretend like I could count on Nic like I could Geraint. Instead, I made myself pull away. I knew next to nothing about Nic, and I didn't want to fool myself into thinking I could rely on him. Of course, it seemed I hadn't known everything about Geraint, either. But honestly, I'd known he wasn't telling me everything about his past, and I'd never pushed. It was easier just to accept what he gave me and not dig any deeper. Really, I was just as glad I hadn't. If I managed to rescue him, I wasn't sure how things would change, but I knew they would. That broke my heart all over again.

"I'm sorry. I have no idea what happened." I scooted backward on the crash mat I'd put down under my silks.

"Perhaps you should stick closer to the ground until you've recovered from the trauma Baz inflicted upon you," Nic suggested gently.

"Maybe." I sighed. "Guess I'll practice my lyra for a while." I didn't even look up at the silks, didn't put them away like I should have. I just got up and walked away.

The day was well into dusk when I went outside, and mosquitos buzzed around me. Crickets chirped and cicadas filled the air with their pulsating sound. I wiped sweat from my brow and trudged to the house.

Nic and Ash caught up with me, falling in next to me and not speaking.

"Ember," Nic said quietly. "I'll help you get your knight back."

I slammed to a stop and spun to face him, anger flaring after my failure earlier. "Why the change in heart?" I snapped.

He twisted his lips. "One, I need your help to get home. Two, it's the right thing to do."

I bit back all my sarcastic replies, took a calming breath, and nodded. "Thank you. When do we start?"

He took a breath. "As much as I'd like to be home tonight, you need rest, and we need time to plan. We'll decide on a course of action tomorrow."

Just knowing we would try took a heavy weight from my shoulders. I wanted to start now, but Nic was right. Right now, I was almost tripping over my feet. I needed rest.

"Robby will be here tomorrow," Ash reminded me. "We probably need to talk with him, and we have to figure out what to tell the cops. We can't keep them looking for you if you're not missing."

"Ugh."

"All of that can wait until you've slept," Nic insisted.

"Okay. I don't know if I'll be able to sleep, but I'll try." My mind raced, jolting adrenalin through me at the reminders Ash had thrown my way.

"Maybe Nic can tell you a bedtime story," Ash suggested.

I frowned, glancing at her and wondering what she was up to.

"I'm a prince of Nightmare," Nic said. "I doubt I know any suitably friendly stories."

"Try." With that, Ash went inside and headed for the room she used when she stayed over at the house, leaving me alone with Nic.

"Now I'm confused," I admitted.

Nic also looked mystified. "Do you think she was serious?"

"I don't know. Come on. I'll at least show you my room."

"Do you still draw?" Nic startled me by asking.

"Yeah, all the time. I even sell some of my art. I'd forgotten I'd shown you my sketchbook."

"I recall you were quite good for an eight-year-old. Of course, I thought you were the best artist in the world." He laughed, keeping his voice low.

"So did I." I shrugged. "Self-confidence has never been a struggle for me."

"Show me some of your newer art."

Taking a breath, and realizing he was going to see a lot of pictures of Geraint, I headed for my room. Nic followed. His presence rubbed against me, velvety soft and cat-like, twining around my legs, rolling up my back and curling around my neck. The only other person who had that kind of effect on me was Geraint. I would have given almost anything to be with my knight right then. At the same time, I wanted to be back in Nic's arms. He made me feel safe. Even if it was just an illusion, I wanted that right now.

I pushed open my bedroom door, shutting it behind us and leaving us in darkness. By memory, I moved to the desk and flipped on the lamp, bathing the room in a soft yellow glow that was enough for me to see by and would hopefully be comfortable for Nic.

"What does it mean that I'm the Nightmare princess?" I asked while Nic studied the pictures Geraint had put on the wall.

"Ultimately, if you don't want the title, nothing. In the short term, it means you can repair mirrors and arches if you have shadow essence to work with and do a few other minor things. Were you to fully accept your place as our princess, you would gain other abilities. That is, obviously, a gross simplification."

"Oh."

Predictably, Nic found the framed drawing of me and Geraint. He tensed, partially melting into the shadowy form he favored.

"Do you need anything?" I could almost convince myself Nic wore some sort of black cloak instead of dissolving like he had.

He twisted, turning his attention to me for a moment. His deep brown eyes were hard with anger. "No. I don't require anything."

"Great." I bolted for the bathroom, shutting the door behind me, and leaning against it.

When I'd been a child at a friend's sleepover, I'd learned that if you burned a candle in a dark bathroom and said Bloody Mary's name three times, she would appear after you put out the light. I'd also learned she'd steal your soul, or maybe your breath, if you didn't turn the light on fast enough to banish her.

I'd never made it work, but it had left me with a healthy respect for mirrors in darkened rooms. I didn't usually look into them when it wasn't light out, but somehow knowing that Bloody Mary was real made it easier, and I looked into the mirror before I turned on the light.

Nothing. Was she watching? Could she only come to mirrors with silver backing? My bathroom mirror was newer, and obviously not backed with silver if Nic couldn't use it to get home.

Letting out a breath I hadn't realized I'd been holding, I shook my head and flipped on the light. My eyes looked sunken and shadowed, my hair was a mess, and I felt like I'd aged a million years in the last week. I just wanted things to go back to the way they had been. Geraint and I had been happy. There were no mysterious men in my life, no nightmares, and Geraint hadn't been imprisoned by one of my childhood friends.

Not having energy for much, I splashed water on my face, brushed my teeth, and went back into my bedroom.

Nic had taken Geraint's rocking chair and pulled it over next to the bed. My heart clenched, seeing someone else in my knight's chair. I didn't make him get up, though. That would be silly.

"You really don't have to stick around while I try to sleep. I can find you a bedroom or something."

"I don't typically sleep at night," Nic said. "And I would not be surprised if you attract the attention of the more powerful dream creatures that have slipped through to the conscious realm now that you've been to Nightmare. I'll guard your rest."

"Oh. Thank you." I wasn't sure how I felt about having him here, but at least I wouldn't be alone.

He nodded.

Since he wasn't leaving, and I didn't want to sleep in the clothing I was wearing, I dug around in my dresser for something to put on. I didn't usually wear anything when I shared with Geraint, and this last week was the first time I'd slept alone in ages. I found one of my knight's longer t-shirts and a pair of short shorts and went back into the bathroom to change.

I was used to showing skin, and I didn't think about what I wore until I came back in the room and Nic's expression heated, gaze traveling up my nearly bare legs. Blushing, I cleared my throat and quickly scrambled into bed, throwing the covers over me.

Rolling over onto my side, I turned my back to Nic and tried to get comfortable in the center of my bed.

"I'm really a Nightmare princess?"

"You really are," he answered.

"Just because we pretended to get married?"

"Nightmare is the essence of imagination and pretend made real."

"You're not happy about it?"

Nic chuckled. "No, not really. Dio was ecstatic, excited we'd get to keep you forever. Baz wasn't upset by the idea. I guess I just assumed we'd choose someone when we were older, and I couldn't imagine you wanting that either."

"Well, I have Geraint," I said a little stubbornly.

"I'm somewhat willing to overlook that," Nic said. "I'm not sure the others will."

"Right," I grumbled. "Kind of not your choice, anyway. My body, my heart, and you three just vanished."

"We weren't supposed to be running around the conscious realm and our guardians discovered our recklessness," Nic answered tightly.

"I take it that didn't go over well?" I attempted to keep the anger out of my voice.

110

"No, not at all." His voice softened in response.

"Sorry about that." I wasn't sure why I was apologizing.

"It wasn't your fault. Really, it was mine. I found the unguarded arch. I convinced Mary to take us through."

"So, what does that make us?"

"Technically, married."

"I was afraid of that."

He laughed. "We can fix some of this, but we will have to be careful how we go about doing it. We don't want to get you trapped in Nightmare."

"Baz mentioned something about being dreambound?"

"Yes. You are dreambound," he said. "You're just not stuck in Nightmare like most mortals that end up in Dream. It's a rare occurrence that mortals cross over into the sleeping world unless someone is actively kidnapping circus performers."

"So, Baz was right? Those girls can't leave?"

"Correct."

I sighed.

"So, if we are to rescue your knight, it is a good thing he's one of us, or he'd be stuck there."

I sighed harder. "I can't believe—"

"You're supposed to be trying to sleep," Nic reminded me.

My mind was still racing, and I had no idea how to get it to shut down.

"There's something I'm supposed to tell you." I bolted upright and turned to look at Nic.

Something about the way he sat in the chair, watching me, or the angle he tilted his head, or the way the shadows swirled around him, something caught at my heart. I gasped, curling my fingers into the soft comforter, not sure what I wanted at that moment. Part of me wanted Nic. I'd never wanted anyone except Geraint before. The feeling thrummed through me like a line on one of my drawings that wasn't quite right, but with a little work could become the focal point of a masterpiece.

"Ember," he whispered, "it can wait until the morning."

I pushed away the rogue feeling and flopped back into my bed, pulling the covers up to my chin. "Tell me a story, Nic."

"Once upon a time," he started.

I twisted around to look at him incredulously.

"All the best stories start that way, or so I'm told." Nic smiled kindly at me.

"Okay."

"As I was saying, once upon a time—"

***

Nic had slumped down in the rocking chair, appearing as a combination of shadows at his edges, and solid toward his center, fast asleep.

The sun filtered through my curtains, and I recalled he said he didn't sleep much at night.

Moving quietly, so I wouldn't wake him, I slid out of bed and went into the bathroom. I took my time cleaning up, showering and all that. I wasn't sure I was ready to face the day.

Nic blinked at me sleepily from the rocking chair when I came back out dressed in yoga pants and a tank top. I was going to get into a lyra even if I couldn't manage the silks yet. Baz would not take that away from me. I needed to work through my feelings. Just not twenty feet in the air.

"You can use my bed," I offered, conflicted about that, but also not wanting him to sleep in a rocking chair.

"Thank you."

I didn't stay to see if he took me up on the offer, heading for the kitchen and a light breakfast.

Ash met me with a mug of coffee, which I clutched. "You're the best."

She nodded. "I know. So, your prince tell you a good story?"

I shrugged and sank down at the table, sipping my coffee. "I fell asleep before he got very far. Something about a ghost and a mirror."

"Well, sounds like it did the job. Are you feeling any better?"

"I don't know, Ash. This is all so crazy."

"Where is Nic, anyway?"

"Asleep, I assume. He said he doesn't really sleep at night, but he stayed up to guard against anything that might bother me."

Ash smiled, and I wasn't sure how to interpret her expression. She remembered I was with Geraint, right?

"What's the plan for today?" I changed the subject.

"Robby will be here any time now. So, make sure he's okay? Get your equipment unpacked? Figure out how we're going to rescue Knight?"

"Okay, sounds good. I'm going to get breakfast and see if I can manage some time in the lyra."

"I'll join you." Ash grabbed a couple of bowls and set about making her semi famous doctored instant oatmeal.

Once we finished, we headed for the gym. The sun had been up long enough to heat the day and bring the humidity up. Fortunately, the gym was air-conditioned.

Ash rigged two hoops while I stretched. I deliberately didn't watch what she was doing. I just couldn't think about it, or I might freak out again.

Then, once I felt limber, I walked over to the lyra, still staring at the ground. I hadn't spent much time in one in the last few months, so my hand callouses were gone. I might get blisters, but it wasn't like my hands were soft, so it wouldn't be too bad.

Ash stepped to the other hoop, mimicking my motions. It was a game we'd played together for years, seeing if we could match the other's movements.

"I'll follow."

My cousin just nodded and put her hands on the hoop, setting up for a basic straddle mount.

Letting my mind blank out of everything but following the shapes Ash moved through, I gripped the lyra, flipped upside down and hooked a leg in the metal hoop.

Ash came up to a basic seat and watched as I mirrored her. When I didn't panic, she flowed through the simplest moves we knew, and I loved her for it. The basics were exactly what I needed. I braced my back against the bar, my feet on the opposite curve, and flipped upside down, inverting my man-in-the-moon pose. My breath caught and my heart sped, but when I didn't fall, and the hoop didn't vanish, I moved into the next shape.

As we transitioned to more complicated sequences, my brain let go of some of my fear, at least where the metal hoop was concerned. It had never betrayed me by vanishing. My confidence grew, and we hooked our knees on the top of the lyra and moved up into the spanset—the strap that held the hoop in the air.

Ash slipped through the middle of the straps, and I tried to follow. The move was simple, but my muscles locked up and I just couldn't do it. It was too much like being suspended in the silks for my traumatized brain to handle.

"Hey, Spark, remember that time I caught you and Knight trying to have sex in your lyra?"

For a moment my brain stuttered with the change of subject, but then the memory surfaced, and I clutched at the lifeline it offered.

"We weren't trying. We were succeeding," I replied hotly, pulling my leg down from the strap and safely back into the metal hoop.

"I really hope you sanitized your hoop after."

I snorted. "You wouldn't use it, anyway."

"Well, no, not after seeing Knight's tight ass perched there and you riding him like you weren't six feet in the air."

I shivered, remembering the combination of pleasure and the burn of pain from that experiment. My knight had kept himself perched carefully on the thin metal hoop, legs dangling, one arm gripping the lyra above. Geraint's rock hard cock had rubbed me all over on the inside, filling me, keeping me firmly in place while I provided most of the motion. We'd ended up in a spin, and finding a position that worked had been giggle inducing. The ultimate answer had been rocking the lyra kind of like a swing. At least until Ash had interrupted, warning us we were about to get caught by eyes far more innocent than hers. My parents hadn't told me about an extra class they'd scheduled. Really, Ash had saved us, but unfortunately, we'd not gotten around to repeating that particular experiment.

Now that time we'd hung two sets of silks in our apartment at one of our contracts...

I shivered again. We'd gotten a lot of use out of some easy suspensions, not to mention Geraint was as good at the splits as I was.

"Well, I guess I should have just brought up sex and Geraint and maybe we could have gotten you out of the silks yesterday without Nic having to do his weird shadow shit," Ash said.

I hadn't noticed myself get down, but now that Ash brought my attention back to the present, I was standing on the ground below my lyra with a serious case of wanting dick.

"Yeah, that worked, but holy crap, I need my vibrator now." I hugged myself, though the reminder that Geraint was beyond my reach felt like a cold splash of water to the face.

Ash gave me a quick hug. "Go see if Robby is here yet. I'll put the hoops away. We'll keep working on this until you're good again."

"Thanks, Ash. You really are the best."

"I know. Now get out of here."

Before I could continue to dwell on the past, I did what she said, hurrying out of the gym toward the house.

CHAPTER 10

Nic

After so many years away, being in the conscious realm both invigorated me and drained me. The constant draw on my energy wouldn't kill me, but eventually I'd run out of all my extra shadow essence and risk getting stranded in the conscious realm. For a relatively powerful dream that could take weeks or months. For a prince, that danger wouldn't manifest for years. In the short term, being surrounded by vibrant life reminded me how much I'd enjoyed coming here as a child, even if I didn't like direct sunlight.

If Baz hadn't freaked out, and if so many other things hadn't happened, I'd have spent more time here over the last few years instead of doing my best to protect the nightmare creatures that had fled Baz's sudden depravities. I had no idea where Dio had disappeared to, shirking his duty to his people, but if I ever found him...

I turned my attention away from the troubles in Nightmare and back to using the shadows to watch Ember while she practiced in her hoop.

Maybe I shouldn't be lurking, watching without her knowing, but it wasn't like I was watching her shower. Though, the sensual way she moved through the poses in her hoop stirred emotions I wasn't sure I wanted to confront.

117

When the guardians had originally told us the silly game we'd played with Ember was binding, I'd been furious. The future was supposed to remain unknown and hidden until we uncovered it. Dio and Baz, on the other hand, were convinced it was the best thing ever—their words. I'd also guessed that Ember might not be so happy about it either, so I'd done research. We could dissolve the bindings we'd placed upon one another, but all four of us would have to be present to do it. That it was possible had alleviated some of my anger until I'd found out we were also forbidden from seeing her again until we were all considered "of age."

Even with that restriction, confronting this situation we found ourselves in would have been much easier if Baz hadn't had a strange breakdown, or whatever had happened, splitting the three of us and driving Nightmare into a dive toward ruin.

Instead of the three of us banding together with the princesses of Dream and fighting the nothingness that was eating away at the edges of both realms, we were fractured. Dream was holding on better than Nightmare, but they were whole. And I couldn't do anything about it stuck in the conscious realm.

My duty warred with my surprising desire for this woman who flowed through her metal hoop as if made of liquid. How any human could move so fluidly, I wasn't sure. Red fingers of jealousy curled through me when I thought of the knight we'd created to keep her safe with his hands on our princess. I knew they performed together from the pictures and drawings I'd seen on the wall in Ember's room. He had no right...

I took a breath. Ash was correct. It was Ember's heart and her body and her choice. Just as I initially hadn't wanted to accidentally be bound to Ember, she had every right to not want to be bound to us.

I'd convinced myself of this until Ember's trauma reared its ugly head and she got stuck. Ash's tactic of distracting her to talk her down out of her reaction was brilliant, but the subject made me see red. I had to back out of the shadows before I stepped from her bedroom directly into the gym and got irrationally angry with the woman who's fault this all was. Not that she'd known. Not that we'd known. Really, it was no one's fault.

Ember had offered me the use of her bed, and I'd almost accepted, though the chair was comfortable enough. A primal part of me wanted to take her up on the offer just to surround her with my own scent and drown out the knight's. Dio would have done it without question.

The rational part of me wasn't feeling especially rational at the moment, but I forced it to take control and I wrenched my thoughts away from my surprising desire to possess Ember, and back to the more immediate problem. Getting home. Freeing the damn knight. Protecting my people. Those were the things I needed to focus on. Not the way Ember's legs had felt wrapped around me when I'd rescued her from the top of her silks, or how having her sobbing in my arms had triggered my protective instincts.

I was going to kill Baz for doing this to her. I'd bided my time long enough, hoping he would come around. Once Ember and her knight were safe, I'd see Baz dissolve into shadow essence, or I'd die trying.

I sensed Ember and Ash come back into the cabin just as another presence neared. I couldn't feel most humans in the conscious realm unless I was directly interacting with their dreams or using my ability to control shadows to remain aware of my surroundings. My connection with Ember allowed me to track her movements as if I were standing next to her. Ash, surprisingly, glowed to my senses, though she was from the waking world. This new person was from the dream realm. I could sense beings

119

from my realm when in the conscious world. At home, it varied by circumstances.

Curious about this new dream, I pulled my awareness back and solidified myself as much as was comfortable, before heading toward the living area of Ember's house.

I'd rested enough.

Ember had her arms around the new dream when I came into the room. I guessed she had no idea this person was as inhuman as her knight. Ash watched, as did Ember's parents.

"Robby," Ember was saying. "I'm so glad you're okay."

"You too, Spark." The man holding my princess was average height and build for a human, distinctive enough as he appeared now with slightly longer wavy black hair and a neatly trimmed beard, but it wouldn't take much for him to blend into a crowd. He was not of Nightmare, or I would have known who he was. This being was from Dream.

I leaned against the doorframe, arms crossed, and waited for him to acknowledge me. There was no way he'd missed my presence.

He held Ember until she released him. My princess wiped a few tears from her eyes and startled when she saw Robby's attention turn to me.

"Ah, uh, Robby, this is Nic."

Robby bowed, low and courtly, with an edge of mocking that only one trained at the high courts could manage. "Your highness."

"Jester," I guessed.

He smiled and bowed again, not as deeply, acknowledging my assumption as correct.

Ember frowned, tilted her head, then her expression darkened. "Is no one in my life normal!" she shouted angrily and stomped her foot.

"No," Ash replied deadpan.

Ember spun around and stared at her cousin.

Ash made no effort to hide the amused smirk on her face.

"Define normal, honey," her mom prompted.

Ember floundered for a moment before gritting her teeth. "Right, I walked into that, but you know what I mean. Here, for clarity, I'll rephrase. Are any of the men in my life human?"

"No," Robby answered, mimicking Ash's deadpan tone.

"I am," her dad said.

"Ugh." Ember threw up her arms and stalked out of the room.

"Spark," Robby called after her. "Where is Knight?"

"Fucking Baz fucking has him." Ember slammed a door.

"Well, I suppose that's better than the alternative." Robby shrugged.

"What!" Ash glared at the jester. "What alternative could be worse?"

"I was half convinced Prince Nic here had killed him already."

"No. I have not yet met Ember's knight." I straightened from the doorframe and came farther into the room, avoiding the shaft of sunlight from the large window.

"Why would Nic kill Geraint?" Ember's dad asked.

"Why indeed," Robby said, tapping his lips with his finger. "I could name several years of reasons." He grinned when my expression darkened. "Ahh, I see not all is forgiven. I had hoped to see that confrontation. Perhaps I'll still have the chance."

I took a calming breath. "Jester, why are you here?"

"Mm, I was on earth looking into things for the court when all the arches vanished and the mirror dwellers disappeared. I've pieced together some of what happened from the few dreams and nightmares that have slipped through the cracks since then, but many details elude me. Shocking, I know."

I snorted. "I'll fill in the details later. I take it you attached yourself to Ember so you could get home?"

"I hoped that eventually she'd facilitate that desire."

I nodded. "Well, if you don't mind going to Nightmare, you might have your chance soon."

"Excellent, though I need to return Spark's plant to her first. She's fond of it."

"You might try apologizing," Ash pointed out.

Robby nodded, amusement dancing in his eyes. "Perhaps. I'll take the plant with me when I track her down."

The jester left, and Ash and Ember's parents all turned their attention to me.

"Yes?" I folded my hands into the shadows that shrouded me like a cloak and tried not to squirm. I was a prince and princes didn't fidget.

"You're not going to try to kill Geraint, are you?" Ember's mother asked. "We all love him so much."

"No. I am going to make him squirm for a while, but it would be silly to help rescue him just to kill him. If I truly wanted him dead, I'd leave him with Baz. Excuse me," I said, shooting a glance at Ash before leaving the room. Hopefully she'd follow after getting rid of Ember's parents. We needed to get back to Nightmare.

I knocked on the door before letting myself into Ember's room. She had curled up on her bed, a blanket wrapped around her shoulders. After a quick glance to see who was coming into her room, she went back to staring blankly at her bed, chin resting on her knees.

"We should plan our rescue attempt." I sat in the rocking chair.

Ember sighed. "How could I have forgotten the three of you?"

"Likely a touch of magic. Someone hid your memories away, but didn't delete them. It just took the right trigger to bring them back."

"Okay, so what are we going to do?" She sounded so small and defeated. I wanted to seriously injure the being that had hurt her. Unfortunately, I was at least partially to blame.

"Ash and the jester should be here shortly. We should wait for them."

"What's a jester?" She huddled deeper under her blanket.

"Robby is a court jester. This means he's an advisor to the high court, the king and queen of all of Dreamland. He's also occasionally a spy, an informant, an actual entertainer, and many other things. I've never met him before, but I knew his predecessor from when I was young. She was quite talented, but went missing about the time everything else happened."

"Everything else?"

"Baz's break with realty, the strange nothingness taking over Dream, the arches breaking, the mirror dwellers vanishing, etcetera."

"Oh." Ember took a breath. "So, things are bad in Dream right now?"

"They're certainly not good," I admitted quietly.

A soft knock warned us before Robby opened the door, a succulent in one hand as he came in. He flourished the plant and bowed to Ember.

"Thank you, Robby," she said, her eyes lighting up. She reached out, and he put the pot in her hand. She actually kissed a petal before stretching out so she could put the plant on the windowsill before curling back into her blanket.

Ash joined us, phone to her ear.

"Yes, dearest. That's perfectly fine. Whatever color you want. Except that one." She paused. "No, I'm joking. That color is fine. I'll pick a few things to match it when I get home. Soon, dearest, very soon. Love you too, bye!" She slid her phone into her pocket.

"How's Stacy?" Ember asked.

"Soon-to-be wifey is doing great. She's planning." Ash grinned.

"Am I still invited to the wedding?" Robby asked, humor coloring his voice.

"Yes, asshole," Ash muttered. "But only if you manage to rescue Geraint."

"Ahh, I thought his Highness was in charge of rescuing the errant knight?"

"You get to help," I interjected before anyone else could answer. "Since you're coming along."

Robby bowed again. "Very well."

"Besides, better that Baz blames you for interfering than me. He can't do anything to Dream, but he's so far avoided terrorizing everyone under my protection. That could change if he thinks I've actively gotten involved." The thought of what Baz might do to my people chilled me, but I attempted to keep that to myself.

Robby gave me a knowing look, but I doubted Ember or Ash had any idea.

"So, what is your grand plan? Do we have a working arch? I assume there's at least one since you got here. Have you found a mirror dweller?"

"Yes, jester, Bloody Mary is still alive. She says a few others are buried deep. Ember repaired an arch to get us here. I'm hoping she can repair two more, get us back to my residence, and then we can sneak into the castle and get the knight."

"And what if she can only repair one?" Robby asked.

"Then we go straight to the castle," I said. "It is more complicated, but doable."

"And how, pray tell, will she get the essence she needs to repair the arch?"

"From me, obviously," I snapped.

"What, is she going to, like, drink your blood or something? Do you have essence for blood?" Ash crossed her arms and stared at me, looking both defensive of her cousin, and fascinated.

"What is it with you and blood?" I raised my eyebrows.

"Ash might have a slight vampire problem," Ember said, caught between amusement and fear. "She's got a good point, though. Also, is there any way to leave the mirror intact? They're so expensive, I hate to leave my parents' mirror broken."

"We should use the cabin mirror," I said. "It will be easier to get into. If you want to repair the mirror over the fireplace without fixing the arch, we can do that before we leave."

"So, shadow blood or…?" Ash prodded.

I sighed, shook my head, and reminded myself that I liked Ash. "I was rather hoping Ember could figure out how to siphon my energy. I suppose if she can't, I could open a vein for her." I kept my expression blank, but Ash looked surprised.

"There are other, more enjoyable ways to share bodily fluids," Robby pointed out.

Ember's eyes widened and her cheeks turned bright pink. "Let's try the siphoning thing, shall we?"

It took a heroic effort, but I kept the amusement I felt off my face and out of my voice. "It'll be easier if we're touching." I held out my hand.

After a moment, Ember put hers in mine and sat on the edge of her bed. Unable to help myself, I brushed my thumb across the back of her hand. She had a firm grip, and she tightened it reflexively when I caressed her.

"Okay," I said before I could get distracted. "You remember the feel of the essence you manipulated before?"

"Yeah. I can even feel it around you."

"Try to draw that into you." I chose my words carefully, trying not to leave any innuendos open for our overly horny audience to pick at.

Ember shut her eyes, and I missed having that soft brown gaze fixed on me. I jerked my mind away from those thoughts, admitting quietly that it might not be just the audience members that were having inappropriate ideas.

She scrunched up her forehead adorably, and I wanted to smooth those wrinkles away from her skin. I wanted to do a lot of things to her and having her hand in mine, having her so close that I could smell the sweat from her workout earlier and how it enhanced her natural odor, was making it very difficult to do anything but think about having Ember in my arms again.

Her growl of annoyance refocused my attention on our present.

"It's there. I can feel it. But it's not responding to me."

Robby snickered.

"Jester," I snapped.

"Sorry, sorry. It's just so easy." He held out his hands placatingly. "Perhaps you need to try harder to share your energy with her."

Even Ash gave him an annoyed look at his amused tone.

Ember actively ignored both of them.

"I'm not stopping her from taking it. It truly shouldn't be difficult for her. We're already bound." Carefully, I attempted to push my essence into her.

"I can feel that." Ember twisted around and glared at the other two when they laughed. "Enough out of you. We're trying to rescue Geraint. Stop."

"Sorry," Ash and Robby muttered, looking a little embarrassed.

"Okay, so I can feel the essence trying to go into me." This time, she snorted. "Sorry. But it's not working."

I clenched my jaw, thinking. I'd really have rather avoided any sort of intimacy unless we were actively choosing it, but she was right. This wasn't working. "Okay." I stood and tugged Ember to her feet. "I'm going to kiss you."

"Probably better than opening a vein," she squeaked.

"Probably," I replied dryly.

By some miracle, our audience stayed silent.

"Okay?" I wasn't going to kiss her if she didn't give me permission.

"Yeah, sure. We need to save Geraint and get you and Robby home. Let's do this."

I hesitated, but the way her eyes softened when our gaze met tugged at my heart. The quick flick of her tongue across her lips just about undid me. I'd intended for this to be a clinical kiss, but I wasn't sure I'd manage that with the raging desire trying to take control.

Ember leaned into my touch when I cupped her cheek with my free hand. She released my other hand, and I put my arm around her waist, pulling her close and leaning over to press my lips to hers.

My princess put her arms around my waist and stepped forward, pressing her chest against mine, eyes fluttering shut as she softened to me.

The storm of emotions inside me raged. I had to protect her, keep her safe, and I wanted nothing more than to tuck her away in a secluded corner of my realm and hide with her. Instead, we were going to sneak into the castle and rescue the man she loved.

Ember gasped as some of my shadow essence flowed into her through our connection. I pressed with my tongue, and she opened, meeting my exploration with her own. She fisted my shirt, which I helpfully made more solid so she could get a firm grip.

I wanted to possess her so badly, yet she wasn't mine. Instead, I did my best to make this moment unforgettable. By her soft moan, I was doing a good job.

Our kiss had gone well past what was necessary to give her a little essence, but she made no move to back away, and I'd take anything she would give me. Desperate didn't even begin to describe how I felt. This was what I'd been missing these last years without her in my life. This connection. This possession. I needed more, and it nearly broke me knowing she loved another.

Someone cleared their throat.

Ember made a surprised sound, as if coming back to herself, and jerked away.

I let her go, heart thudding in my chest.

She met my gaze for a moment before blushing and looking away. "Sorry," she muttered.

I took a breath and nodded. "Nothing to apologize for. That worked, didn't it?"

"Yes, I think so." She ran her hand through her shoulder-blade-length hair and pulled her bottom lip between her teeth. "Right, so, uh, when are we leaving?"

"As soon as we decide on the rest of our plan, should we have to go directly into the castle," I replied.

"Okay, yeah, um, what is our plan for that?"

I glanced at the jester. He shrugged.

"We'll try to stick to the shadows," I said. "Easier for me, but I can shield you if we hide in the shadows that lurk in the ceiling."

"How exactly are we going to do that?" Ember's eyes widened, and I wanted to kill Baz all over again. She'd never been afraid of heights before.

"I won't let you fall, Ember," I said, reaching out and brushing my fingers along her cheek. "I promise."

CHAPTER 11

Ember

I'd wanted back in Nic's arms before, but holy crap, I wanted my hands back on him now, with his lips on mine, his energy flowing into me. The shadow essence curled through me, making itself at home, pushing against parts of me I hadn't known existed. It was as if I were being expanded from the inside. My awareness of the world around me grew, and that included my awareness of Nic. I almost wished I'd kicked everyone out of my bedroom and taken the time to change into clean clothing, but I hadn't wanted to admit how much just getting kissed by the Nightmare prince had turned me on. I didn't even want to admit it to myself, but it was kind of hard to ignore the wet panties and the way my heart still thudded in my chest.

Some part of me knew he was already mine, and I was already his. Maybe the part of me that combined with the energy he'd shared, filling an emptiness I hadn't known existed until it was no longer there. Was it because of my silly childhood game?

Honestly, if my three childhood friends hadn't vanished from my life and memories, I'd have fallen for them, anyway. Instead, they'd sent me Geraint. Who I apparently wasn't supposed to fall for. Seriously, how could I not have? Geraint was apparently made specifically for me. Thinking back on our time together, it really was telling how easily he fit into my life. I had just thought it was because we'd grown up together with similar interests and all. Now, well, it was a lot more obvious Geraint literally lived for me. Damn it. Now I was questioning if he even liked me. Was it all duty? Now I had an idea of why he'd resisted for so long when I'd wanted to move beyond friendship. Fuck. Had I forced him? Did he secretly hate me?

The emotional turmoil was more than I could take, and I wrenched my thoughts away from my feelings and tried to focus on our mission. I hid my face and wiped away a few tears. Nic put his hand on my shoulder and squeezed, but didn't say anything.

Neither of my parents were in the living room when I went in to repair the mirror. I was just glad there wouldn't be an audience beyond what I already had. I felt a bit like a mother hen with three needy chicks following me around.

That my manager was some sort of dream court jester was blowing my mind, although maybe not as much as Geraint being some sort of actual knight from Nightmare. Putting all of that and the rest of my distress out of my mind, I stepped up on the brick hearth and touched my hand to the mirror.

"What do I do?" I glanced at Nic.

"I don't have the power to repair mirrors and arches. You do. Remember what you did when we were running from the hounds, and do it again," Nic answered.

"Right, just that easy," I muttered. He was correct, though, which didn't make me any less annoyed. I shut my eyes and pictured the essence flowing between the cracks in the glass, making it whole again. The energy Nic had shared with me left my body through my hand, flowed through the mirror, and a smaller amount returned to me.

When I opened my eyes, the mirror was whole once again. Now that I had a tiny bit more experience, I could feel where the silver backing was still fractured, and the connection to Dream broken. Bloody Mary could still get through, so I guessed that meant that mirror dwellers could look out of even broken mirrors, but no one else could use the glass as a gateway. I even thought I knew how to fix the arch. Unfortunately, repairing the mirror had used up more than half of the energy I'd taken from Nic. That could be a problem.

I'd address it with him once we were at the cabin. Right now, I needed to say goodbye to Ash and my parents.

Stepping off the hearth, I went over to Ash and held out my arms for a hug. She squished me tight. "Be careful, Spark."

"You too, Ash. Can you make sure my parents take care of my plant while I'm gone?"

We released each other.

"Yeah. You're coming back here after you get Knight, yes?"

I nodded. "Yeah, we'll be back."

"Good, because I need to kick his ass for keeping this from us." Ash smiled, but I caught the shine of tears in her eyes.

I gave my cousin another quick hug before turning away.

"Your parents are in the gym," Ash said as I headed for the front door.

Nic eyed the sun streaming through the front windows and sighed. "I will meet you at the edge of the woods."

"You really can't do a little sunlight?" I had to ask again, though I had seen him walk across the lawn in the sun once already.

He stuck his arm into the shaft of sunlight. It didn't burst into flame, but the sun leached all the tawny color from his skin, and he looked like a black and white painting. "I can. I can even appear normal when forced, but it takes a great deal of energy. If we're going to confront Baz, I should conserve as much energy as I can. It's easier simply to step from this shadow to the ones in the forest."

"That's really cool," I said, then a thought occurred to me. "Hey! Is that how you always found me when we would play hide and seek?"

His lips twisted into an embarrassed smile, and he cast his gaze to the ground. "That might have something to do with it. My range is much farther than when I was young."

"Explains why I did occasionally manage to hide from you."

Nic chuckled. "Yes."

"Okay, go lurk in the forest. I'm going to hug my parents, promise them not to die, and I'll meet you there in a few."

The prince nodded and stepped back into the shadow behind him, dissolving into black wisps of essence before vanishing.

"Holy shit," Ash breathed.

"Most impressive," Robby agreed. "Let's find your parents. It's been too long since I've been in Dream, and I'm eager to get there. Even if it's the darker side of home."

I glared at Robby. "Yeah, let's get right on that."

He smiled, tilting his head. "I want Geraint rescued, too, Spark. I also want to see him squirm when Nic tells him how naughty he's been."

Shutting my eyes and clenching my jaw, I tried to keep my temper. "Robby," I snapped.

"Yes, princess?"

"Shut up."

He chuckled and gestured for me to precede him out the door. I sighed and remembered why it had taken me so long to warm up to our manager in the first place. I wondered if Geraint had befriended him because he'd had no other choice.

The walk to the gym stretched as I dragged my feet, trying to take in all the details of my home. The vibrant flowers in the garden I had yet to tend, the forest I hadn't explored since last summer, and it looked like I might be missing the summer camp. Hopefully, Casey would call and pick up one of the instructor's positions.

"Spark," Robby said, voice soft. "It'll be okay. Nic won't let anything happen to you, and neither will I. You'll be back before you know it."

I glared at my friend, wanting to lash out at him. Really, what had he done wrong? Nothing. That didn't make me any less annoyed.

Turning my back on Robby, I power walked toward the gym. *Fine. Let's get this over with.*

The cool air chilled my skin into bumps, and I rubbed at my arms when I came inside. I looked around for my parents and paused, watching as they danced. I so rarely got to see them perform together anymore, and I didn't want to interrupt.

Robby put his arm over my shoulders like he always used to, and I didn't make him move.

The energy between my parents, the sheer connection of a lifetime of dance together, took my breath away. They spun and twirled each other, moving to a waltz. I remembered that they'd talked about adding ballroom dance to their class list this summer.

"You and Knight have the beginnings of that synergy," Robby whispered.

"Do you think he's okay?" I replied.

"No, but I think we'll rescue him, and he will recover." He side-hugged me. "Don't be too hard on Knight, Spark. He did the best he could."

135

"I just don't even know what to think now," I admitted.

"He loves you."

"But…"

"Geraint loves you with all his heart. And it's not just because they created him to keep you safe."

I tried to object again, but Robby cut me off. "Enough, Spark. He loves you. We'll sort out the rest later. Yes, you two need to talk, but the bigger problem is what to do about the princes."

"What about them?"

Robby smirked at me. "You're technically married, and you've been sleeping with the hired help instead of your husbands."

"That's BS and you know it."

He laughed. "I do, but they don't. You may have to protect Geraint from their baser instincts once they figure out how close the two of you are."

"Nic knows," I whispered as I watched my parents finish their dance. Dad pulled Mom into his arms, and they stared into each other's eyes before kissing.

Robby didn't answer. I glanced up at him, but he had a faraway look in his eyes, so I didn't press him. Easier just to let it go for now.

Mom and Dad saw us and came over.

"Are you leaving?" Mom gave me a worried look.

"Yeah, we need to rescue Geraint." I twisted my hands and stepped away from Robby.

She pulled me into her arms. "Be careful, honey. If I could keep you here, I would, but I know nothing will separate the two of you for long. I'm just glad he was able to help you escape in the first place."

"Yeah, me, too." I tried not to let any of my doubts color my voice.

Dad took over the hug. "This is all so unreal. If I hadn't seen you come out of a mirror, and the strange things your friend can do…"

"Trust me, I feel the same way," I mumbled into his shoulder, trying not to cry.

"Come home to us, Spark," Dad said.

"I'll be back before you know it." I stepped away from my parents and let Robby lead me from the gym. I'd spent hundreds of hours in that gym, and it felt as much like home as the house did. I hated leaving, but I told myself I'd be back soon, and I'd have my knight with me.

Tears blurred my vision, and I hurried across the expanse of the yard toward the shade of the trees in the surrounding forest. Robby kept pace with me, and by the time we reached the shelter of the canopy, I'd gotten my emotions under control. As much as I could manage, anyway.

Nic stepped out of the shadows and fell in next to me as I found the overgrown path to the old cabin. We didn't talk, and I focused on my surroundings.

Insects buzzed through the air, and after I found a spiderweb with my face, I remembered to grab a long stick and wave it in front of me. The trees thickened into the forest I'd played in as a child, and a quiet calmness settled over me. This was home. This was where I belonged. Geraint and I had talked about doing a photo shoot out in these woods with our silks and straps and maybe even lugging the lyra out here. Promo shoots was our excuse, but really, we just wanted to play our favorite games in our favorite environment.

We hadn't gotten to it yet, but we'd always said we would. Then summer got busy, and then we were leaving for our next contract. This summer we were getting our pictures. I'd make it happen. Somehow.

The forest had encroached on the cabin since last I'd been here. The roof still held, and the walls were strong, but if that old tree that towered over it lost a few limbs, the cabin might get destroyed.

Nic stood behind me while I studied the old structure. His presence curled around me. Unconsciously, I took a step back until we were touching. Nic put his hands on my shoulders, and I placed one trembling hand over his.

"Aww, you two are so cute," Robby said in a falsely sweet voice.

"Jester, it won't take much for me to forget who you are and put my fist through your face," Nic growled.

Robby gave the same mocking bow he'd given Nic earlier today, and Nic's fingers momentarily dug into my shoulders before he relaxed.

"Are you ready, luv?"

"Yeah, I think I know what I'm doing, but Nic, I used more than half the energy you gave me just repairing the mirror."

"Hmm," he replied. "That might make it difficult to repair two arches."

"You'll just have to give her more essence." Robby made an obscene gesture.

"Yeah, I'm going to punch you, too," I snapped.

"Oh, you two are way too serious about this. Kiss and take us to Nightmare Castle. We'll rescue the knight and escape into the countryside. It may take a few days to find another mirror you can repair, and in the meantime, Nic can give you the tour of your kingdom."

I turned to face Nic, and he put his arms around me.

The shy smile I gave the prince was almost as embarrassing as the way my stomach tightened and my heart raced at the thought of kissing him again.

Nic brushed some hair out of my face. "Sorry."

"Why?"

"I'm enjoying kissing you far more than I feel I should."

"Oh." I blushed. "It's okay. I don't mind."

His smile was sheepish, and I wished I'd said something smoother. Instead of trying to find better words and tangling myself up in them, I put my arms around Nic, getting used to the way his body shifted under my touch unless he put effort into being more solid. I kind of liked it. It was different, but I also liked that he put in the effort to remain stable for me. It made me wonder what sex would be like.

Oh shit. I'd just gone there, hadn't I? It felt like a forgone conclusion that we'd be sleeping together at some point. I really needed to get myself under control. If nothing else, I already had Geraint, and I wasn't willing to give him up. Unless that was what he wanted. We needed to have a talk we'd both probably rather avoid. It was easier just to leave things the way they were. Unfortunately, that was no longer possible.

"You're thinking awfully hard, Spark," Nic said, jolting me with his use of my nickname.

"Sorry."

"We have a lot to sort through, Ember. Let's tackle one thing at a time."

"You're right. Sorry," I repeated.

"No need for apologies. I don't mind." He winked at me when he echoed my words back.

That made me laugh, which might have been his goal. He was smiling when he bent over and kissed me.

I clutched at his shirt, pressing against him, not even trying to hide my embarrassingly needy moan as I opened for him. Nic was a fantastic kisser. Maybe it was a nightmare guy trait because Geraint had always been good at it, too.

139

Nic tightened his grip, clutching me against his chest, making his own pleased sound as our tongues danced.

I accepted more essence from him while we kissed, as if my body knew what to do with it now, and wanted more. I still didn't think it was enough to repair two arches, though. One, yes, but not two. Thinking at all was getting difficult and my hands wandered, almost as if of their own volition. While I'd been thinking about shadow essence, I'd unclenched my fists from Nic's shirt, and now my hands cupped his ass. He couldn't have minded, because his body solidified under my touch, instead of dissolving into shadow.

Changing my clothing would have been a wasted effort. I was well and truly turned on, my nipples hardening into points as I rubbed against Nic's chest like a cat in heat.

This time Robby didn't interrupt us, and we kissed until my head was swimming and I had to pull away with another needy whimper.

I should have felt worse, making out with Nic while Geraint was in danger, and before we'd talked, but it felt so fucking right to be in the Nightmare prince's arms.

Nic's eyes were shut, and he'd pulled his bottom lip between his teeth, as if trying to rein back powerful emotions.

"Think you can get us there?" he asked, voice rough.

"Yeah." My voice was equally husky.

For a wonder, Robby kept his mouth shut. Maybe a small sense of self preservation?

I turned away from Nic and headed for the cabin. The prince and the jester followed. I jiggled the handle just right and pushed open the door.

A layer of dust coated everything in the cabin, and something scurried across the floor. No one had been in here since we'd cleaned this place out as kids, and it showed. Otherwise, it was an exact replica of the cabin in Nightmare, other than the differences in the mirror.

This one wasn't cracked, however, and I wondered if I might be able to repair both arches with the amount of essence I had. Nic's mirror probably was shattered though, and I didn't think I had enough to fix that, as well. Stick with the plan, go to Nightmare Castle. It wasn't the last place I wanted to go, but it was close.

"You've got this, Ember," Nic said.

"Yeah, okay, what do I do?"

"Since the mirror is unbroken, just call Mary. We'll tell her where we're going, and she can direct us. Same as before."

"Just say her name three times?"

"Yes," Nic replied. "No candle required."

I laughed.

"I've always wanted to meet the infamous Bloody Mary," Robby said. "The mirror dweller who typically assisted us folks from the lighter side of Dream was the Lady in White."

"Isn't she a ghost?" I was familiar with that legend.

"Yes, but many ghosts, especially those with a great deal of belief behind them, dwell in mirrors when they're not off haunting mortals. Some even haunt mortals in the mirrors as well."

"I think I'm looking forward to this tour," I admitted.

Nic squeezed my shoulder.

"Okay, let's do this. Bloody Mary, Bloody Mary, Bloody Mary." I looked deep into the mirror and held my breath, nervous even though I'd met Mary before.

When I had to take a breath, I frowned and glanced at Nic. "Isn't she usually here by now?"

"Let me try," he said and took my place in front of the mirror. When Mary failed to appear after he repeated her name three times, we all shared a concerned glance.

141

Dakota Brown

"What happened to Mary?"

"You said she's the only mirror dweller active, correct?" Robby asked.

"Yes," Nic replied.

"What if dear old Baz grew angry with her for helping your escape?"

"Shit," Nic muttered. "I hadn't considered that."

"Do you think he hurt Mary?" I covered my mouth, worried about the terrifying woman who'd helped us escape.

"He won't have hurt her too badly," Nic said. "Imprisoned is more likely. He'll need her to move around if he wants any of his people to get to the conscious realm."

"How do we get back, then?" I hated how my voice broke.

"Prince Nic will simply have to use his princely ability to take us home after you fix this arch."

"There will be no way to hide my involvement with rescuing the knight," Nic said grimly. "There will be repercussions."

"What ability?"

"Even without a mirror dweller, I can activate an arch to get us home to Nightmare. It only works with the main travel mirror in Nightmare Castle, simply because that's where the magic is strongest, and it takes a great deal of effort. It's a one-way thing. I can get home, but I can't go to other places. A failsafe so the princes don't get stranded somewhere they don't wish to be. I could still become trapped here, but not easily."

"Ahh. Well, at least we can get back. Right?" I knew there had to be more to it than Nic said, but it didn't seem as if we had any options, either.

He nodded. "There is that. Okay, let's get home. Ember, if you would please fix this arch."

I moved as carefully as I could, trying not to stir up too much dust. Unfortunately, there was a lot. One sneeze set off another.

Nic came up behind me, wrapping shadows around us, until I could breathe again.

"Thanks." I rubbed at my nose and made it the rest of the way to the broken mirror without incident.

The broken glass was cool under my palm. Nic was still touching me when I pulled on the essence, channeling it through the cracks. Instead of taking the energy inside me, I accidentally grabbed onto his instead.

"Yes," he breathed. "That's how you siphon."

"Maybe I just needed to be actively using it."

"Perhaps."

With his much larger well of energy to draw from, fixing the mirror was no trouble at all. It took me a little longer to fix the arch, but the effort was minimal once I figured out how to feed the shadow essence through the fractures.

"Good job, Spark," Nic praised me.

His pleasure rolled through me, filling me with warmth and desire.

"This will not be like your last trips through the mirrors. The transition will be much more abrupt and jarring. Jester, be ready should there be someone standing guard on the other side of the mirror. It is possible they're expecting us."

Nic put his arm around my waist, and Robby put his hand on Nic's shoulder. I curled into Nic's embrace and buried my face against his chest, feeling weak but not wanting to watch, just wanting to feel safe.

Nic's shadowy presence wrapped around me, and his powers jerked us through the mirror so rapidly, I barely felt the liquid cold splash as we passed through the glassy surface before we tumbled out the other side.

Nic kept us on our feet. I risked a look, and Robby made it seem like he did this sort of thing every day, standing with a sword he'd pulled from somewhere in hand, gaze scanning the empty room.

At least, I thought it was empty.

Nic dragged me back into the shadows, and Robby followed until we were heavily concealed. This had to have been a ballroom at some point, but dust coated the surfaces and dirt dulled the mirror, much like the rest of the castle.

Robby took a deep breath. "It is good to be home," he whispered. "I wasn't sure how much longer I'd be able to hold out."

"Then it is a good thing we found each other," Nic replied equally quietly. "The doors are guarded from the outside. We must take to the shadows. Do you have any skill in that regard?"

"I'm a jester. Of course I do." Robby grinned at Nic. "What about our princess?"

Nic glanced at me. "She'll have to trust me."

I nodded, not brave enough to speak, but willing to do what he wanted.

"Wrap your legs around my waist and your arms around my shoulders, and hang on."

He supported me while I did what he instructed. The move wasn't difficult. I'd done it many times over the years with Geraint. Nic was slimmer, but just as strong.

"If you have to shut your eyes, it's okay," he said before moving through the shadows, using them to slide up the wall and into the shadow essence that had always hung thick on the ceilings when I'd been here just a few days before.

It wrapped around us, concealing us from view.

Robby moved differently than we were, and I lost track of him quickly. He blended in with the surroundings like he had some sort of cloaking device from a sci-fi movie. For all I knew, he did. When the doors opened, Nic was ready to slip through them. I guessed he would have had an easier time leaving the room without me hindering him.

The guards outside looked around, but, seeing no one, went back to their blank, gray-eyed stare.

The shadows that lurked along the ceiling were thicker than I'd expected, easily hiding us from view with room to spare. Nic crawled through the black mist, fingers sinking into the substance, or possibly melding with it. I couldn't be sure. He crawled as if he were a spider on the ceiling, but through the shadows instead. I lay on his chest, legs and arms wrapped around him, head resting on his shoulder and staring below us, feeling detached from reality. Of course, I was in the land of dreams, so that tracked.

"Are you doing okay, Spark?" Nic whispered.

"Yeah, I think so. You?" I almost asked him if he was hanging in there, but decided it probably wasn't time for joking. A handful of the weird gray guards passed beneath us, and I tightened my grip on Nic. He remained mostly solid, grunting softly when I clamped down, but my legs sank into his waist a little.

We weren't alone, so I didn't apologize, not wanting to risk someone overhearing my whispers. That my harsh pants hadn't already given us away was some kind of miracle.

"Not far," Nic whispered, voice tight with the strain of carrying me through the shadows. Or maybe he was simply unhappy about the entire situation.

The hallway narrowed as Nic took us down a side corridor. He paused and moments later I heard the clatter of boots on stone.

Nic went rigid, barely breathing, and I tightened my grip further. Baz, followed by an entire group of those gray-people guards, stomped into view.

As if trying to give me a heart attack, Baz jerked to a halt and spun around, staring back the way he'd come—the same way we were going.

"That damn knight," Baz snarled. "If we didn't need it for bait to draw that bitch back, I'd end it now."

Fury roared through me, and I practically saw red. I must have moved, ready to launch myself at Baz and claw his eyes out, if nothing else. Shadow tendrils wrapped around me, fastening me to Nic and covering my mouth so I couldn't let loose the snarl of rage barely contained behind my lips.

"Shh, luv, rescue the knight first, revenge later," Nic whispered in my ear.

Trembling in reaction, but knowing Nic was right, I tried to settle against his chest while we hid. Even knowing who Baz was, I still felt no recognition when I looked at him.

Baz snarled at the gray man standing next to him for a bit longer, then spun on his heels and stormed off, the gray people following.

Nic finally took a full breath.

"He can't see us up here, can he?"

"He should have sensed both myself and the jester, not to mention you."

"Really?"

The shadowy prince nodded and resumed his crawl through the black mist.

Icy fear crept along my spine, replacing the passionate fury that had warmed me. What had Baz done to Geraint? Was he okay? What kind of trap had Baz laid and what were we about to walk into?

I was about to find out.

CHAPTER 12

Nic

It took most of my self-control to keep certain parts of my anatomy from letting Ember know exactly how much I enjoyed having her cradled against my chest while I worked my way through the shadows.

What I wouldn't give to possess her heart like the knight did. Nothing about the anger I'd felt when I'd found out about us being bound by our little game had me prepared for the complete desire I had for her now.

She shifted her position, and I made myself focus on melding with the shadows and staying out of sight. A task that was as natural as breathing and required next to no attention.

"Nic," she whispered in my ear.

Bloody hell. I couldn't hide the shiver that trembled through me as her breath tickled my skin.

"Yes, luv?"

"Are you okay?"

"Fine. We're here." I supposed I hadn't answered her when she'd asked me a few minutes ago. Grateful I could distract her from that line of questioning, I studied the hallway below us.

"Baz mentioned a trap." She continued to torture me with the feathery touches of her lips on my skin.

147

"The jester is investigating. I don't sense anything through the shadow essence."

The dream being stepped from wherever his abilities had hidden him and gestured for me to come down.

"Hold on," I whispered.

Ember's grip tightened. She was so incredibly strong from her lifetime of aerial that my ribs protested, and I had to soften my body a little to compensate. She squeaked.

"I won't let you fall," I assured her, wrapping a few tendrils of shadow around her. She loosened her grip, and I lowered us to the ground, using the wall to steady myself while I held Ember against me. Oh, how I wanted to turn and shove her back against the wall, with those muscular legs wrapped around me…

I jerked my attention away from how good her body felt pressed against mine and helped her stand until she adjusted to being on her own two feet again. The jester shot me a knowing look. I narrowed my eyes at him, and he held out his hands placatingly.

Ember stared at the door as if she could sense her knight behind it. Maybe she could? It wasn't out of the question, but I didn't want to know the answer.

"Is it strange that they don't have a guard at the door?" Ember asked, twisting her hands together.

"Not necessarily. It depends on how easily they think you can find your knight. There are many places to stash prisoners in this castle." Uneasy, but unable to figure out why besides the current situation, I acknowledged the feeling and set it aside.

"It depends on if they already know you're involved or not, your highness," the jester said. "It appears they don't, in which case they're expecting Ember to come in the front door, as it were, instead of through the mirror, as they have Mary neutralized for the moment. They may not realize how she escaped and think she's still wandering in Nightmare and they're hoping to lure her back."

I nodded. "Probably. It should be obvious to Baz that either myself or Dio have gotten involved, but so far it doesn't seem like he's figured that out. Very odd."

"As I am a mere jester and not royalty like the two of you, I will take the risk of opening the door."

I motioned for him to proceed.

With a mocking bow, the jester went over to the door and put his hand over the keyhole.

"Be careful, Robby," Ember breathed.

"Of course, Spark," he replied, much more seriously.

The click of the tumblers was loud in the silence. Ember clenched her fists. Robby pulled his hand away from the lock and tugged on the iron ring. The heavy wooden door creaked open.

I didn't even have to look inside to know Ember's knight was in terrible shape. She covered her mouth with her hands, and her skin blanched.

"If you will allow me to give an order," the jester said. "You should remain outside. Just in case."

I inclined my head as regally as I could manage under the circumstances.

"Go on, Spark," Robby said.

She rushed inside, the jester following closely.

The door slammed shut, because of course it did.

"Shit," I muttered, and melted into the shadows just as shouts echoed down the hallway.

The guards rushed past, and I shuddered at how gray and lifeless they all appeared. When last I'd resided in Nightmare Castle, all the dream beings that lived here had been lifelike with their own imaginations and essence. The creatures that streamed past me were the barest imitation of what had once lived here. What was Baz up to, anyway? Beings like this had no chance of standing up to the more

149

powerful dreams that might try to step into reality, no ability to negotiate or bring them over to an understanding of how they might exist both in Nightmare and in the conscious realm. Their primary function had always been to protect the conscious realm against powerful nightmares, not run around and play army for Baz.

Speaking of, Baz stormed down the corridor, shoving past the weird dream beings and slamming to a halt in front of the magically closed door. That I still couldn't discern the magic he'd used to trap Ember inside worried me. I should have been able to sense anything Baz could manipulate.

He stared at the door. A slightly more animated-looking guard approached, bowing. "What is your wish, your highness?"

"I should leave them in there to rot," Baz growled.

It took effort not to spring from the shadows and slide a blade pulled from my imagination through Baz's throat. The trouble was, the animated guard carried a ray gun, and those things were bloody hard to deal with. Science fiction fans everywhere had created that particular addition to the dream realms. The edged weapons the lesser guards could conjure weren't much of an issue.

"Now that we have the princess, we can dispose of the knight," Baz continued.

For half a second, I was sorely tempted to let him follow through with that, but the heartbreak that would cause Ember pushed the impulse from my mind. I was not, however, ashamed that I'd thought it. She was supposed to be mine, to share only with my brothers. Instead, we'd lost her completely to a mere knight.

"Open the door and get her out," Baz ordered.

The guard opened it and went inside, dragging a wide-eyed Ember out. The ray gun to her head likely had a lot to do with her lack of struggles.

"Hello, Princess," Baz said slyly. "I didn't appreciate your last game, but from now on, we'll only play the ones I like."

Ember shuddered.

I'd seen enough. I slipped from the shadow that hid me, to the one across the hallway, right behind Baz.

He stepped closer to Ember, reaching for her. I grabbed his shoulder, digging my fingers into his flesh and yanking him backward, my conjured blade going to his throat.

"Hello, brother," I hissed. "Let her go."

Baz tried to jerk out of my grip, and my blade sank into his flesh. He froze. "You'd kill your brother over her?" He sounded surprised.

"Yes."

"You won't escape the castle if you do," Baz said.

"I think you overestimate your shadow of a guard. We can find out if you like?"

"Release her," Baz ordered, anger tightening his voice.

"I'm not leaving without Geraint," Ember insisted when the guard that held her shoved her away.

"I've got him," the jester said, coming out of the cell with one of Geraint's arms draped over his shoulder, supporting most of his weight.

Though made of dream essence, the knight had essentially been human for so long that I wasn't entirely sure he would survive the abuse Baz had inflicted on him without assistance. Many of his bones looked broken, and even as out of it as he was, he clutched at his ribcage. He hobbled on one good leg, the other twisted where no joint should have been. His bare skin was bruised and bloodied, and I wasn't exactly sure what color his hair should be, or what his normal skin tone was.

Tears glistened in Ember's eyes, and I tightened my grip on the blade at Baz's throat. Even if we had to fight our way out, we could escape after I killed him.

"Nic," the jester said, holding out a hand, face tense.

Clenching my jaw, I refrained, barely, from murdering my brother. It wasn't just the jester's words that kept me from doing it. There were other consequences from killing a prince of Nightmare. If nothing else, there were meant to be three of us, and killing Baz early might trigger the next cycle—in which new princes or princesses of Nightmare would be cultivated. It might not, though, and I was almost angry enough to risk it.

Turning Baz by the grip I maintained on his shoulder, I marched us toward the nearest exit.

No one spoke, and the shuffle of feet on the stone floor drowned out the pounding of my heart and Ember's soft sobs.

It wasn't long before we reached one of the side exits. "Open the door," I ordered the guard. He complied, and I dragged Baz outside of the castle.

The jester followed with his burden, and Ember was right behind him.

"Just to make sure we get away," I growled at Baz. "You and I are going to have a little chat. Jester, get them out of here. I'll catch up."

"Yes, your highness." There was no mocking this time, just compliance as the jester led Ember and her knight away from the ruin that had come over Nightmare Castle.

My heart clenched, watching them go, but when Ember stopped and looked back at me, a tiny spark of hope eased the pain in my chest. Concern narrowed her eyes and creased her forehead, as if she didn't want to leave me behind. Maybe not all was lost.

"I thought you were content with your corner of this wretched land," Baz said.

"Just biding my time, Baz. The consequences for your actions are coming due." I tightened my grip on my asshole brother.

"You—" His words cut off in a gurgle as I pressed harder with my blade.

"Just stop before I decide to see what happens if I slit your throat."

He didn't reply, but he also didn't push the issue, and I settled in for an uncomfortable wait. I wanted to give Ember and the jester a reasonable head start before I slipped through the shadows and joined them. While I waited, I considered options for our escape plan.

CHAPTER 13

Ember

"Geraint," I whispered once we were away from the castle.

He groaned in reply.

"Later, Ember," Robby said.

"Is he going to be okay?" *Please let him be okay.*

"If Nic will help him once he catches up with us," Robby adjusted Geraint's arm over his shoulder. "Now help me get him as far away as we can. Once Nic catches up, we won't have long before Baz sets his troops on us."

"He has hounds," I said, voice shaking with the memory of being chased.

"Even better," Robby muttered. "Get your arm under Knight and help me."

"It'll hurt him."

"Better us hurt him than we get caught by Baz's hounds and they hurt all of us."

"Damn it," I grumbled and did what Robby ordered. Geraint smelled of both old and fresh blood. He really needed a shower, but that was the least of my worries right now.

The last time I'd fled the castle, I'd hidden in shadow. This time, nothing obscured me from the rest of the land, and we caught a lot of attention from barely seen creatures in the darkness. We followed a path through a thick wood

155

full of twisted trunks and reaching branches. Hints of color shone through the shades of blacks and grays. It wasn't dark. It was more that it simply wasn't very light out. My eyes adjusted, but I tripped on the occasional branch. Each jolt made Geraint groan, though that was preferable to nothing at all given the situation.

Eyes glowed in the darkness, blinking and staring but not approaching. A few globes of light hovered off in one direction, but after nearly falling into a bog the last time I was here, I didn't fall for the will-o-the-wisp's lure again.

I didn't have the breath for questions, and I didn't have the energy to worry about anything other than my knight, and I hoped Robby would know what to do if something attacked us.

The leaves rustled and a darker shadow slunk through the trees.

Robby quickened his steps, but Geraint cried out in pain, and we had to stop completely as he collapsed.

I fell to my knees next to my lover and simply refused to look into the darkness. *This is how you stayed safe, right?*

Something yelped in the forest. Branches cracked and snapped.

I whimpered and focused on Geraint. Robby stood over us, and I relied on him to protect us.

"It appears you've attracted some attention."

I shrieked, jerking around, but it was only Nic, stepping from a shadow, though he seemed to take a lot of it with him as he appeared more shadow than man as he approached.

"Nic," I breathed. "You're safe."

"Yes, of course." He kneeled next to me and studied Geraint, a frown wrinkling his brow.

Nic then glanced at me, clenched his jaw, and came to some sort of decision. I wasn't sure what caused the sadness that clouded his eyes for a moment, but he put his hands on Geraint's chest and pushed essence into my knight.

I could sense the energy transfer, but it didn't seem like Geraint was accepting it.

"Maybe he's been gone too long," Nic said. "Most dream creatures can't survive in the conscious realm for more than a few days or weeks at a time unless they're a powerful manifestation. Vampires, for example, and werewolves and a few of the more popular cryptids have a great deal of power because of the huge number of people that dream of them. They're some of the exceptions, surviving for months or years, or even never returning to the dream realms once they reach the waking world. Your knight was specially created to survive in the conscious realm."

The shadowy prince leaned back and studied Geraint. I could feel the essence curling through my knight, trying to join with him.

"We can't linger long," Nic said softly, his hand going to my shoulder.

Tears blurred my vision. If we couldn't save Geraint, then what was the point? I put my hand on my knight's arm and willed what little essence I held into him.

This seemed to go better, and I grabbed Nic's arm. "Can I?"

"Go ahead." He sounded resigned, and I wondered why. Would this hurt him?

Still, he'd given permission, so I shut my eyes and pulled the essence from Nic and shoved it into Geraint. The energy flowed through me and into my lover, melding with the essence Nic had already shoved into him and curling through his body. He took so much, but finally I could tell we'd given him as much as he could hold.

I released Nic.

The prince sagged forward, sinking his fingers into the dirt, panting. "Nic?"

"I'll be okay, Spark. See to your knight."

He had faded mostly to shadow, and I couldn't make out his features. Uncertain if I should worry or take him at his word, I went with the easy route and turned my attention to Geraint.

My partner's color had vastly improved, and the bruising faded. His bones no longer looked broken. Old blood still covered Geraint, but he breathed easier, and after a minute or two, his eyes snapped open.

He looked first at me, and he heaved a relieved sigh. "Spark," he breathed, his familiar Irish lilt banishing some of my fear.

I nodded, unable to speak for the lump in my throat. He wiped a tear from my cheek, then jerked his hand back when Nic cleared his throat.

Geraint paled again. "My liege," he said hesitantly.

"We need to get out of here." Nic stood, ignoring Geraint.

I got up and offered Geraint a hand. He accepted, and I pulled my partner to his feet. It broke my heart that he didn't tug me into his arms. Instead, he shot a wary look toward Nic before glancing over at Robby.

The jester looked ridiculously happy, though I wasn't sure if it was because Geraint was back on his feet, or because of the tension between Geraint and Nic.

"I've requested mounts." Nic interrupted the awkward silence. "Until they respond, we will have to go on foot. We've lingered in one spot long enough."

I grabbed Geraint's hand and tugged. I couldn't help it. I needed to be touching my knight. He didn't pull away, but the normal familiarity of his touch was missing with the stiffness of his grip. If the situation hadn't been so dire, I'd have made Nic and Geraint talk it out now. Except there were many things we hadn't even begun to sort out. So maybe it was better to wait.

"What will we do if nothing responds?" Robby asked Nic. "How far does Baz's reach extend?"

"We are still well within the territory he controls, but there is little loyalty to Baz. More, it's fear that motivates those who dwell under his thumb. Who is strong enough to risk repercussions? And how badly will my people suffer because we rescued the knight?"

Geraint's hand tightened on mine, but he didn't say anything.

"We should head for the border," Robby said. "The modern monsters should be strong enough to stand against Baz, what with all the strength they've gained with the monster fuckers and their vivid dreams."

"What?" I sputtered.

Nic chuckled. "It surprised them, too," he explained. "It started with the vampires, years back. They became popular and their home territory shifted slowly from deep in the darkest realms of Nightmare to the neutral boundary between dreams and nightmares. They've been in that middle ground ever since.

"Monsters gained a certain popularity more recently, and their shift was far more instant. One day, their home territory existed well into Nightmare, and the next, they're overrun with all the dinosaurs that live in the boundary lands."

"Dinosaurs?" I squeaked.

"Yes, as with many things, movies and books made them popular. Some already resided in the boundary because children and scientists have always been fascinated by them. However, ever since those movies came out about the dinosaur parks, they have overrun the boundaries."

159

"Wait, did you say that the monsters' territory just moved? Because people want to, uh, have relations with them?" I finally said, lamely.

"Yes. The lands of Nightmare and Dream are ever changing based on the human imaginations that give these lands their form. The boundary between the lighter and darker parts of the realm is the only solid feature besides Nightmare Castle, and Dream Castle, and yes, I know, those names are very eighties cartoon," Nic explained.

I laughed.

"So we head for the boundary. If we make it that far, then we can cross into Dream. We'll be safer there. The dream arches aren't broken, but unless we can find a mirror dweller, we're stuck here," Robby said. "It's possible The Lady in White is hiding out in the neutral boundary lands."

I snickered. I couldn't help it.

Nic glanced at me. "What?"

"You have a neutral zone."

He blinked, then shook his head. "I suppose that is the case."

I knew he got my reference, and the faint smile on his lips made me think I'd amused him.

Geraint sighed quietly, and I looked at my knight. He released my hand, avoiding my eyes.

Crap, what now? I did not want to confront any of this. I wanted everyone to be happy, and I wanted everything to work out. Not knowing what to do to make things better was killing me.

We hurried down the trail for a while in silence, before Nic stopped and tilted his head, as if listening. Robby looked behind us.

"We're about to have unfriendly company," Robby pointed out.

"Yes, I know," Nic snapped. "Keep moving. I'll be back." Before any of us could object, he vanished into the shadows.

Robby took the lead, increasing his pace. Adrenalin and fear warred with a creeping exhaustion that had snuck up on me unaware. I risked a glance into the darkness. The eyes still watched us, and the shadows shifted unnaturally, but nothing came out of the gloom to attack us or help in our escape.

Geraint took my hand and urged me to move faster. I was glad to be touching him again, but the distance in the contact tore at me. *Damn it.*

"Where is Prince Shadow?" A low voice lisped.

I ran into Robby's back when he halted. Four immense wolves stepped out of the woods, eyes gleaming in the weird ambient light, fangs practically glowing white against their black fur.

"What the hell," I gasped, instinctively curling into Geraint's arms. He let me stay there.

"We come at the prince's request." The lead one forced the words through lips that weren't meant to utter our language.

"Ahh." Robby bowed. "Our thanks."

"I'm here," Nic said, stepping from another shadow. "I diverted the hounds for a time."

The lead wolf dipped his head. "What is our objective?"

"The boundary," Nic replied without hesitation.

"Wise," the wolf agreed. "I will carry our princess."

Oh shit, we are riding giant wolves?

Geraint, looking nearly as unhappy at the prospect as I felt, tugged me forward. The massive creature kneeled.

"Are you sure?" I asked.

"It will be my honor," the wolf growled. He held out a leg for me to step on.

Not wanting to anger the wolf, I buried my hands in his thick fur and stepped up onto his leg. My years of performing with Geraint helped me mount the wolf gracefully, carefully climbing up his side and swinging a leg over his back. I even managed not to squeal in terror as the creature stood, forcing myself to trust him, as I would have trusted my knight. Or Nic.

The wolf had a broad, muscular back that wasn't uncomfortable, simply strange. His muscles bunched under me, and I clamped my legs around him and held tight to his coarse ruff fur.

I looked at the others. Robby had climbed onto the back of another wolf and Geraint approached a third. Nic had his hand on the shoulder of the last, a smaller wolf that rested her head against Nic's side. He dug his fingers into the creature's fur. Perhaps he knew the wolf well? They acted very familiar.

A twinge of jealousy curled through my body, surprising me. Where had that come from?

To distract myself, I turned my attention to the wolf that would carry me. "Do you like being pet, or do you prefer I keep my touch minimal?"

"You may pet me, Princess. I am honored by your attention, and it pleases me. Others may lose a hand."

That startled a laugh out of me. "Do you have a name?"

"You may call me Ghost. Hang on, Princess. We run."

I clutched Ghost's fur as he and the others leaped into a rolling lope. Nic and the smaller wolf led, with Ghost following behind her. Geraint and Robby rode to either side and slightly behind me, all of us running in kind of an arrow shape. It didn't escape my attention that I was in the center of the formation.

Riding a giant wolf through the wilds of Nightmare was an experience I didn't even know how to describe. First off, I was riding a wolf. A huge, horse-sized wolf with canines the length of my arm. Their ground-eating gaits were not uncomfortable, as long as I trusted Ghost. Simply an amazing and new experience.

The deep forest closed in around us, and the endless shine of blinking eyes stared from the darkness. I shivered and nearly pitched over Ghost's head as he slid to a stop.

Two young girls blocked our path, eyes solid black, wearing light blue dresses. They both dragged giant axes, dripping blood.

"You cross our path," they said with the same voice, slightly out of sync. "You must appease us."

"We travel to the boundaries," the lead wolf growled. "Give way for your prince and princess."

Their dead black eyes shifted from Nic to me. I clutched at Ghost's fur and tried not to show how terrified I was. Surely two axe-toting children were no match for a bunch of dire wolves.

That Nic's wolf backed into Ghost when the children stepped forward did not comfort me.

"We give way for the princess, that she may save us from the nothingness. We will take the price of passage from the pursuers."

"Jesus fucking Christ," I swore quietly as they stepped into the darkness. The wolves took up their run, maybe just a little faster than before, not slowing until the trees thinned.

We broke out of the dense forest and onto vast grasslands. I looked up into the gray sky, tinged with hints of blue. Clouds drifted lazily on an unseen breeze, and I marveled as they shifted from cloud shaped, to dragon shaped, to fish shaped, and through many other patterns. I

163

couldn't explain it, but suddenly the clouds froze as if noticing someone watched them.

Unable to look away as the clouds shifted back into cheerful puffy forms, I clenched my fingers on Ghost's fur. The familiar cumulus puffs should have been reassuring. Instead, fear trickled icy fingers down my spine. Moments later, eyes slitted open on the clouds, and gashes like mouths gaped at me, filled with jagged teeth.

My jaw dropped open, and I mewled in terror as the clouds dove out of the sky toward us.

At my frightened squeak, Nic followed my gaze and sighed in exasperation. The wolves slowed.

"Stop. You can terrorize us all later," Nic snapped.

The clouds paused.

"Promise. We'll give you a good round of chase once Baz's hounds are no longer after us."

I gaped at Nic, then at the puffy clouds as they seemed to confer, before shifting their attention away from me and toward something behind us.

"Yes, go chase the hounds, good idea."

The clouds zoomed away.

"Holy shit," I breathed and glanced over at Geraint. He looked as shocked as I felt, and I reminded myself he hadn't spent much, if any, time in Nightmare before coming into my life.

Robby shook his head. "Even your clouds are terrifying. Very nice," he said dryly.

Nic ignored Robby.

Our mounts took up their lope again. Ghost gave no signs of tiring, despite his tongue lolling from his mouth and the way his sides heaved under my legs from his exertion. I unclenched my fingers on one hand and risked patting him on the shoulder. He flicked an ear in my direction, and I swear his mouth opened wider into a grin.

Grateful he was happy to carry me, I took a breath and tried to get my racing heart under control.

Off to our left, the grasses bent and swayed.

Something flashed across our path. The wolves slowed to an easy trot.

"Hunt the hounds trailing us, instead," Nic ordered, sounding amused instead of fearful.

The grasses rustled as whatever it was did as their prince commanded and raced away.

"Is anything here not terrifying?" I patted Ghost again.

"We are all terrifying," Ghost growled. "We are Nightmare."

"Right. Okay, that was a dumb question," I muttered.

Robby laughed. "Spark, just wait until you see Dream. You'll be wishing for a return to simple Nightmares. Dream is a twisted place."

"You might be surprised at how quickly dreams transform into nightmares," Nic added. "And not all nightmares are simple, just as not all dreams are twisted. It's a complicated land. If you stayed, you'd never truly get used to it, but you'd grow to love it."

Could I grow to love it here? I'd just been threatened by clouds with teeth, and creepy twins, and something hidden in the grass. What was next, scary corn fields? They'd left us alone when Nic had told them off, but still...

I pet Ghost again as the wolves went back to their ground-eating lope and quietly admitted I looked forward to meeting some of the other residents of Nightmare. I was also worried about Mary and the other mirror dwellers. Not to mention the dreambound women Baz had abducted. I wondered if there was something we could do for them.

And then there was Nic. The shadowy prince that was helping Geraint, even though he didn't want to. He did that for me. He'd mentioned that he hadn't been happy to find out our childhood game had real consequences, but the way he'd kissed me had me thinking he might have changed his mind.

I looked over at my knight. How were things going to change between us? Could we survive this challenge? Did he even want to be with me? Robby assured me that Geraint loved me, but that didn't mean he wanted to share my bed anymore.

Ugh, this was such a freaking mess.

"Ghost, how far are we from the boundary lands?"

"Not far," the wolf replied.

I tried to take in the surroundings instead of wallowing in my thoughts, though now that the clouds had left and nothing seemed to stalk us through the tall grasses, there wasn't much to see.

After a time, the wolves slowed. The gradual transition from mostly gray scale, with splashes of color, to a more vibrant landscape, caught me off guard. I stared at vivid colors, marveling at them, before I realized that the scenery had changed. The color palate was still not quite what I was used to, as if someone had taken out all the subtle shades and simply left the primary colors—purple was one shade of purple, green had no variety, and red was starkly arterial red. Risking a glance up, I studied the sky. Robin's egg blue stretched ahead of me, with a few white puffy clouds floating through the air.

"Shadow Prince, where do we go from here?" the wolf Nic rode asked. Her voice was higher, possibly a female.

"We seek The Lady in White," Nic said.

The wolves grumbled and yipped amongst themselves before the lead wolf spoke again. "We do not know where she has hidden. We suggest you ask the succubi and incubi for a guide."

Ghost shifted under me. "I sense a nothingness storm," he growled. "We must shelter."

"A what?"

Ghost didn't answer my question. Instead, he bolted after the lead wolf. This run felt almost frantic, especially compared to the easy lope before. Even the edge the wolves had displayed after meeting those creepy twins was nothing compared to how they ran now. The trees rustled as wind gusted around us. Birds or some other bird-like creatures burst into the sky and flapped away with raucous cries.

The lead wolf yipped.

"Ember, create a den, or a cave system, or something for us to hide in," Nic called urgently.

"Me?"

"You're our princess. You have the power of creation in this land."

"Why, because I'm female?" I snapped.

"No, because you're human, with a human imagination. Dream and Nightmare are formed from human dreams. That's why you can repair arches. If you were male or any other gender, it would be the same."

"Oh." I had not considered any of that. "Okay." I squinted, imagining with all my might that we were about to come upon a large cave system similar to the one on my property, but giant and wolf-sized, that would shelter us from whatever storm had everyone in a frenzy.

We raced around a bend and the very cave system I'd just imagined waited. The wolves didn't hesitate, heading straight into the mouth of the den I'd created for us. We ducked low to avoid knocking ourselves out.

"Ember, make sure this is safe from the storm," Nic ordered, slipping from the back of his wolf and heading toward the entrance. He pulled shadows from our surroundings and capped the opening, plunging us into darkness.

"I imagined it would be safe from the storm," I said hesitantly, voice quiet.

"Then it will be," Nic assured me.

"You could imagine us some lights," Robby suggested dryly.

I shut my eyes and thought. The first thing that came to my mind was hundreds of fireflies dancing through the air, much as they did in our forest at home.

"That's something, at least," Robby said.

When I opened my eyes, thousands of fireflies danced around us. The wolves eyed the tiny lights suspiciously for a moment before accepting that the glow was harmless.

I did my best to keep my imagination in check. I didn't want to create some sort of weird firefly monster.

Geraint and Robby dismounted. Geraint took a step toward me, then glanced at Nic. The shadow prince currently had several dozen fireflies circling his head. He held up his hand as if he were going to swat them away, then dropped it and came over to my side. I wasn't sure if he'd noticed Geraint's hesitation or not.

I let Nic help me off Ghost, though I probably could have managed it on my own. Then I gave Ghost a big hug. "Thank you for carrying me."

He nudged me with his muzzle, nearly knocking me over. "You are welcome, Princess."

"Okay, what's a nothingness storm?" My eyes were adjusting to the low light of the fireflies, and saw that fear tinged the anger that crossed Nic's expression.

"I believe I mentioned the nothingness before. It's like the land is being erased and the storms bring the disease that eats away Nightmare. It's dangerous in other areas. I've kept you out of the worst of it, but it appears the boundary is getting hit now."

"But we'll be safe here?"

"Yes, because you imagined this as a haven for us," Nic said. "Otherwise, I'm not sure how it would affect you. Those of us fully of this realm would probably have ceased to exist. They come up suddenly and unpredictably."

I hugged myself, shuddering. "That's awful. Has it always been like that?"

"No. It started about ten years ago," Nic replied. He put a hand on my shoulder.

"And no one knows why?" I let him pull me into his arms, conscious of Geraint's eyes on me.

"No. We've been too busy dealing with Baz, and then Dio vanished. Perhaps someone in Dream knows more."

"How long do they last?"

"Hours. Sometimes days." He hugged me. "You should get some rest, Ember. You've done a lot today."

"Do I need to imagine up a bed?" The idea of sleeping on the hard ground was not appealing, but Nic was right. I was exhausted. Hopefully, we wouldn't be stuck here for days, though.

"Use the essence instead of your imagination," Nic said.

"Okay." Making the shadows do my bidding was getting easier, and I pulled it into a soft mat, much like I'd slept on in the castle. I lay down and glanced at Geraint. He looked about ready to drop, so I held out my hand to him. We always slept together and, despite the way he smelled, I wanted him back in my arms. I probably reeked too by now, and I just didn't care.

Geraint hesitated before sighing and looking away.

"Lay down, knight, before you fall down," Nic ordered. "You do none of us any good if you are too tired to fight."

Geraint bit his lip before lying down on the edge of the mat, not touching me. He curled up on his side, back to me.

I shut my eyes, but I was too tired to deal with any of this right now. One wolf laid down on the other side of my knight and pressed into him. I shifted so my back was against my knight's, and Ghost lay down on the other side of me, partially on the mat, squishing us together. I quickly warmed, surrounded by musky wolves.

Geraint had fallen asleep almost instantly. It took me longer. Just as I drifted off, I heard Robby ask Nic, "What are you going to do?"

"She's in love with the knight. What can I do?" The pain in Nic's voice tugged at my heart.

"The three of you meant to share her. What's one more?"

Sleep claimed me before Nic replied.

CHAPTER 14

Ember

Sometime in the night, both Geraint and I had shifted until I was cradled in his arms, wolves pressed against our backs, my head resting on my knight's shoulder. Except for the wolves, this was how we normally slept, and waking in his arms settled everything in my mind. At least for the time being.

Wolves snored loudly, and when I stretched my leg, I bumped into someone else. It didn't take much movement to see that Robby had curled up at the end of the mat. I didn't see Nic, but some sense of him made me think he stood over by the entrance.

Fireflies danced above us, and the air had warmed considerably and staled slightly.

"Is the storm over?" I whispered.

Wolf ears flicked toward me, but the creatures stayed asleep.

"Yes," Nic answered from the direction I'd sensed him. "We have time. Get some more rest."

I let my eyes flicker shut, since it was obvious no one else was ready to wake. Truthfully, I didn't want to move from Geraint's arms, afraid this might be my last chance to be held. My entire life—the perfect life that Geraint and I had worked so hard to build—was changing by the minute, and I didn't like it. What would happen to our business? Not to mention, what would happen to us?

My knight tightened his arms around me, as if sensing my distress. He reflexively kissed the top of my head and threaded his leg through mine before going still again.

Tears sprang to my eyes, and I let them streak down my face, quietly displaying my pain to any that would notice in this dark, firefly-lit cave.

Crying myself to sleep was not my favorite, and waking up with my eyes glued shut by sand was even worse. To top that off, I was no longer cradled in my knight's arms. Ghost still lay against my back, but otherwise, I was alone.

I scrubbed at my eyes until they were clear and slowly climbed to my feet. Sore muscles protested, and my thighs ached from riding Ghost.

Nic had cleared the shadow door from the entrance, and it looked like everyone but Ghost had left the cave I'd imagined for us.

"Thank you for warming my sleep," I said to the wolf.

He nodded and shoved his enormous head under my hand. Laughing, I scratched behind his ears and gave him a big hug.

"Are you coming with us to find these guides you suggested?"

He shook his head. "They are not far, and we must discover the extent of this storm's damage."

"What could possibly want to destroy the dream lands?" I wondered as I headed for the exit.

"We do not know. You cannot exist without us, and we do not exist without you," the wolf said.

"Holy crap," I breathed as I stepped out of the cave. It was as if someone had taken a giant swath of gray and smeared it across the landscape. The only thing wasn't awash in gray was the cave I'd created. Though even parts of that were erased away. We might not have been as safe as Nic had suggested we were, but we'd survived, so I guess that was something. Hopefully, there wouldn't be a next time, but if there were, I'd do better.

The other three wolves, Geraint, Robby, and Nic, stood nearby, surveying the damage.

"Will this ever recover?"

Nic shrugged. "So far, no. Perhaps if we were at full strength, us with our princess, and the Dream princesses with their prince—who they have not found yet. As it is, Nightmare is fractured, and Dream can't find their prince without access to the conscious realm."

"Wow. Okay, so you have to have mortals? Why?"

"To keep the energy in the realms fresh," Nic said. "Before you ask, it has nothing to do with reproduction."

"Oh."

"There are always three princes or princesses of Nightmare, same with Dream. The combination of genders is variable, and occasionally their gender is also fluid. The one they choose to be their mortal fourth usually carries the title of princess or prince based on the bearer's preference, but not always. Especially in your case, they made assumptions."

"Gotcha. So, we need to go find succubi. Aren't those like sex demons or something?"

Robby laughed. "Yes, they are. But they're also fairly universal nightmares and dreams, so they travel both realms extensively. They are the tour guides of the dream realm, if you will."

I tried to wrap my mind around that and couldn't. "Let's go then."

Nic quickly thanked the wolves for their help, and I gave Ghost another scratch before we headed off toward the edge of the blight that had erased the land.

We walked in uncomfortable silence that Robby broke with a jaunty whistle. He was enjoying the heck out of something. Probably Geraint's tension.

I wanted to make everything better, but couldn't think of what to do, so I just trudged along. It took longer than I thought it should to reach the end of the smeared landscape. Walking into the flat color tones of the boundary lands was a relief. I'd have been happy to be back in the nightmarish forests after that stretch of nothing.

My fingers itched to take Geraint's hand. Or even Nic's. Hell, I'd almost settle for Robby's hand at this point. I did not like this unsettled energy between us. I watched my knight for a while. He alternated between shooting worried looks at Nic, shooting worried looks at me, and staring at the ground. Then he'd act like he remembered he was a guardian and survey our surroundings before starting over again.

Nic walked along like he didn't have a care in the world, and he ignored Geraint other than the handful of commands he'd given yesterday.

Robby kept whistling that same song over and over.

The landscape alternated between dense forest, serene valley with a flowing stream in the middle, and craggy mountains, seemingly placed at random. There was no logic to our surroundings. The only thing that saved us from having to scale mountains was a path that wound through the whole chaotic patchwork. We stuck to the path.

No one bothered us, unlike our trek through Nightmare. Occasionally I saw quaint settlements. Other times cities loomed, complete with vehicles and flying cars. For a while, I watched the changing landscape without realizing how quickly it moved compared to the speed we walked.

When it hit me that I observed the countryside and cityscapes as if I were speeding along in a car, I stopped, frowning.

"The magic of the road," Nic supplied when he turned toward me.

"Weird."

Nic nodded and gestured for me to continue, though I doubted he found the road strange since he was used to these bizarre lands.

We walked for maybe a couple of hours and covered distance I couldn't fathom. Finally, Nic led us from the path. I almost expected some sort of jolt as we slowed down to a normal pace, but the transition was smooth, imperceptible even.

The village, I guess you could call it, that we walked into looked like a cross between a spaghetti western's idea of a town full of brothels and actual homes and businesses.

Beings shaped like humans—female, male, and androgenous—wandered the streets in various states of dress or undress. The style of clothing varied from a woman in full Victorian costume except her ankles were showing, to sexy pirates, to strippers, to women wearing men's shirts and nothing else, and men dressed in tight jeans and flannel, or barely there boxer briefs. There were styles of dress I'd never seen before and hairstyles and body ornamentation I wasn't familiar with. Not only did styles vary, but body types varied as well. My mind reeled, trying to take it all in and sort it out.

We were looking at manifestations of people's sexual fantasies taken form by succubi and incubi.

Nic held out his hand for me to take. Trying not to see the hurt in Geraint's expression, I accepted and let the prince bring me to his side. Nic had taken on a mostly solid form at the moment, though his edges still faded into shadows that wavered around him like mist.

175

We attracted attention almost immediately, though the beings left us alone.

Nic led us to a fancier hotel. Robby darted ahead of us, pushing open the door and bowing as Nic strode past him with me on his arm.

The lobby mimicked an upper scale hotel in the conscious realm. I'd even been in a few very similar. Except all the mirrored surfaces were shattered.

Geraint trailed behind as we went straight up to the desk. A bored-looking woman greeted us. At first glance, she was attired as you might expect the front desk clerk of an upper scale hotel to dress. But when you paid attention, her shirt was too tight, gaping at the buttons over her ample breasts, her skirt was too short, and the stockings she wore were clearly attached by garters.

She straightened from her bored slouch when she recognized Nic.

"Your highness," she said. "How may we serve you?"

"We require a suite of rooms, fresh clothing, and a guide."

The busty blond nodded. "Right away, Shadow Prince." She smiled at him coyly, and I did my best not to let the jealousy raging through me show.

Nic glanced at me and put a hand over mine. *Oops*, I'd dug my fingers into his arm.

She handed Nic an old-fashioned key, dragging her fingers over his in a way clearly meant to entice. "Your guide will be by in a few hours. Clothing for those who need it is already in your rooms."

"Thank you," he said.

My vision went red, but Nic led me away before I could explode. "It's their nature, Spark. Ignore it."

Geraint's agonized expression at Nic's use of my nickname cooled my rage. *Damn it all, anyway.*

We squeezed into an elevator that had every appearance of being modern and in the enclosed space I could smell just how amazingly we reeked. Nic, maybe not, but the rest of us were sweaty, bloody, wolfy, and dirty. I felt gross, and I had no desire to look into a mirror. Even the broken ones on one side of the elevator walls.

The car dinged, and the doors slid open. Geraint slipped out ahead of us, glancing both ways down the hallway before stepping aside and letting Nic and I come out of the elevator.

The hallway was deeply carpeted, and the fixtures were shiny and expensive. I didn't hear any sounds and guessed the soundproofing was also fantastic. I wondered if the succubi and incubi actually lived in these rooms, or if this really was like a hotel for the beings that lived in the boundary lands.

Nic led us to a room, opened it with the key, and gestured for all of us to go inside.

I stepped away from him, doing as he instructed.

"We should be safe here," he said as he locked the door behind us. "Pick a room, for the love of all that is olfactory, take a shower, and meet back here. We have a great deal to discuss."

Robby went to the closest room. Geraint headed to another, and I counted doors. There were only three rooms.

A quick glance at Nic let me see him twist his lips in annoyance. "As I said, assumptions. Perhaps you should take this time to speak with your knight."

"I don't even know where to start, Nic." I hated how lost I sounded.

"Perhaps you should remind him how you feel about him and go from there." Nic's voice softened.

I looked at Nic, confused. *Aren't I supposed to be practically married to him? Why does he want me to remind Geraint of my feelings?*

"I have no claim on you, Ember, no matter how I might feel. Your heart is your own."

"Okay." Why didn't that sit well with me? Did I want Nic to claim me? I shivered at the thought, so yeah, pretty sure I wanted that. The memory of his lips on mine heated me up all over.

I'd get over it. Geraint was more than enough for me. He always had been, and he always would be.

I turned away from the prince and went to the door Geraint had chosen. I knocked quietly, then entered. The rooms were set up like standard fancy hotel rooms with attached baths. The shower ran in the other room and the remains of Geraint's clothing were on the floor by the bathroom door. He hadn't shut it. I shed my clothing and dropped it on the pile of rags that had once been a nice pair of pants. Steam filled the bathroom, and I stopped just on the other side of the door. My knight stood with his back to the stream of water, head hanging down, water slowly cleaning off the blood.

"Geraint."

He jerked up, eyes wide. "Spark," he breathed my nickname as if it were the air that gave him life. His gaze roamed my naked body.

"Are you okay?" We hadn't had even a second alone to talk.

"I am in surprisingly good condition, considering how I felt when you rescued me." Confusion colored his voice.

"Oh, Nic and I healed you somehow. You were in really shit shape."

"He healed me?"

"Yeah. With my help. Guess you've been in the conscious realm too long, and we had to filter the essence through me to get your body to recognize it." Or at least that is what I thought we'd done.

Geraint opened his mouth, shut it again, and looked away, twisting his hands together.

"Mind if I join you?"

"You're always welcome, Ember." He sounded so sad it was killing me.

I slid the glass door on the shower open and joined him under the stream of hot water. I'd intended to keep up the conversation, but the water felt so good it distracted me.

"Okay, let's do this after we get clean." I reached blindly for the soap.

Geraint put a bar in my hand. Then he turned me so my back was to the water, his touch gentle, hesitant, but familiar and very welcome.

My knight ran his hands through my hair, wetting it, while I scrubbed myself with the bar of soap. The shampoo and soap weren't our scents, but the setting was familiar. We showered together often.

I let him clean my hair, gently running his fingers through the strands and untangling the knots. Then I took the bar of soap and scrubbed his chest.

"You need to shave." I chuckled as I played with his beard. He normally kept it neatly trimmed or neatly scruffy, depending on the show season. "You're going to look like a mountain man here in another day or two."

He smiled. "I'll do that if this place has a razor."

"Only if you want to, Knight. It's your choice."

He grabbed my hand and held it against his chest. "You like it neat. I don't have an opinion on it, so I'll shave if I can find a razor."

I took a breath. "Geraint…"

He interrupted me with a kiss.

For half a second, I almost pushed him back so we could have the talk I'd been working up to for weeks now. The desperation in the way he clutched me against himself shoved that thought away. If nothing else, he clearly wanted this, and so did I. I was aching to be touched, to be held, and claimed.

The water cascaded down on us as we came together. There was nothing elegant about our kiss, just pure desperate need for each other. How could I have doubted that he wanted me? He might have been created to be my companion and my guardian, but we'd been together long enough that it had to mean something to him.

The way his hands explored my body, squeezing my ass, kneading my back, furthered my conviction that he wanted me. He knew every inch of me better than I did.

Geraint shoved his leg between mine, his hard cock pressing into my stomach. I ground on his thigh, moaning needily.

My lover kissed his way along my jaw before nibbling gently down my neck. When his lips reached the base of my neck, Geraint bit down hard.

I yelped in surprise, shuddering in reaction. I didn't hate it at all, and he got rough with me sometimes, but we usually discussed it first. I hadn't been expecting him to go there this time.

"I want him to see that when he takes you," Geraint said, voice harsh. "He may get to have you, but I was first."

"I'm not sleeping with Nic," I gasped.

"No?" He clearly didn't believe me.

"Why would I lie about it, Geraint? I've never kept anything from you." *Shit, that just slipped out.* I hadn't meant to bring any of that up.

"I had no choice," he snapped.

"Geraint, I know. It's fine. I'm sorry, I didn't mean it like that."

He was still hard, and I ached for him to fill me, but the way he was looking at me now, I wasn't sure he

180

wanted to be with me. Had I misread the desperation earlier?

"So, now that you know you're sleeping with the hired help, how's that feel?" he bit out.

"Are you trying to push me away?" Inexplicably, I still held the bar of soap, and I sort of threw it at him. Except we were still pressed together, so it was a pretty lame throw.

"You should walk away," he said, ignoring the soap. "If Nic doesn't kill me for overstepping, one of the other two will."

"Nic healed you, dumbass. He also helped me rescue you. He'd figured out we were together, and he still helped. I don't think he's planning on killing you after he went through all that to get you out of Nightmare castle."

Geraint pulled his leg from between mine. I growled at its absence. Instead of giving me what I wanted, my knight shoved me around until my chest was pressed against the cold tile. Then he kicked my feet apart, holding me so I didn't slip and fall. He pressed his hard cock against my ass.

"And you think he's going to let us stay together after this?" Genuine curiosity mingled with the anger in Geraint's voice. "Because I don't want to live without you. It's actual possible I literally can't."

My knight reached between my legs and rubbed a little more roughly than he normally did. He shoved his fingers into me, and I gasped, squirming while he stroked me on the inside.

"Yes," I gasped out. "I'm pretty sure that's his plan." I mewled as Geraint made good use of his talented fingers. He brought me right to the edge before pulling his fingers away.

I cried out in frustration.

"Geraint—" I ended his name in a squeak as he slammed his cock into me. "Fuck…"

"If you want me to stop, tell me." His voice was carefully neutral now, like he didn't care.

"Geraint," I tried again, gasping as he thrust into me from behind. "Yes, fuck it, I want you. I've never stopped wanting you, even when I found out about Nightmare and Nic and the rest. You're the love of my life. How could I not want you?"

"You're in love with a being created for you," he pointed out.

"Well, if you think about it, that should have been an obvious outcome of the situation," I said, though the building pressure in my core was short circuiting my brain. "You are literally perfect for me." I cried out as my orgasm hit me. We almost never went for more than a day without having sex. I couldn't imagine how Geraint was holding out, but he didn't stop thrusting into me, and I squirmed on his cock, too sensitive.

Geraint put a hand on my shoulder, holding me still, shoving me down to meet his thrusts.

"What I need to know," I gasped, "is if you actually want me? You may be perfect for me, but am I actually what you want?"

"Of course I want you," he gritted out, voice breaking. Either he was close to coming, or he was fighting off emotion. "Even though I know it's going to get me killed, the only thing I want is you. I want you crying out my name while you writhe on my cock. I want you flying in my arms as we perform. I want everything we've had together, but that's all going to change now, isn't it?"

My body contracted as I came again. "Geraint," I shouted.

"Yes, Spark?"

"I want everything we have, too. Please give this a chance to work itself out."

He pressed his chest against my back, his beard prickling my neck as he leaned in, his lips going to the other side of my throat. "We'll see. Don't get your hopes up." He bit me again. This time I expected it, and I arched backward, accepting the pain. It sent jolts of pleasure all the way to my core where Geraint filled me.

"I love you," I said when he went back to kissing my neck instead of leaving his mark on me.

Geraint froze for a moment, before resuming his thrusting a bit more gently. He dropped his hand to my clit, stroking.

"Shall we try for three?" he asked, almost playfully now.

"Three's a good number," I murmured, head swimming from the mix of endorphins and emotions swirling through me.

The pressure in my core built to a precipice. "Geraint," I said urgently. "I'm coming."

He sent me over the edge and stiffened, gasping as he spilled himself inside me. I trembled in my knight's arms, and he held me until I had a chance of standing on my own without falling over.

"I love you too, Spark," he finally whispered.

CHAPTER 15

Geraint

Memories

"Don't do it, Knight." Robby sipped his fruity drink and stared at me while I stared at Ember. She flirted with a couple of guys shamelessly.

I tightened my grip on the whiskey I nursed, but I couldn't tear my eyes away from my spark.

"Let her have her fun with other mortals. The princes will come for her soon enough."

"You said something had broken the pathways."

"Arches," Robby corrected automatically.

Realistically, I knew next to nothing about the Nightmare lands where I'd been created. My only purpose was to keep Ember safe however I could. Unfortunately, she didn't know that and couldn't understand why I kept turning down her advances.

It wasn't that I didn't want her. It was just that Robby was right. But watching her flirt with mortals, even if she were just looking for a one-night hookup, was twisting me up inside.

Knowing she'd never been with anyone before made it even harder to let her go off with some random guys in a beachside bar. What if they hurt her? What if they didn't treat her properly? Or what if they actually knew what they were doing? Another voice whispered in my mind, reminding me I'd not been with a woman just as she'd never been with anyone before.

"Something is preventing me from getting home and has been for several years. That doesn't mean I'm not correct. The princes will come for her, and if they find out you've touched their princess, they'll kill you."

I gritted my teeth. "It might be worth it."

"Knight—"

"Jester," I bit back at him.

"Fine," Robby said, downing his drink and holding up his hands. "If you want to sign your own death warrant, then by all means, do so. You'll be breaking her heart one way or the other. Just try not to do it more than once."

He pushed away from the bar and stomped away, probably off to search out his own hookup.

I finished my whiskey, paid our tab, and went to collect my spark, my reason for living, and the woman I'd die for.

"Ember," I said sharply.

She glanced up, tilting her head curiously at my tone. She'd made it into one of the men's laps.

"We have early rehearsal. Let's go."

She opened her mouth to object, and I raised my eyebrows and gestured toward the exit.

"Fine."

"Hey, man, lay off. We were just getting to the good parts," one man said.

"Sorry, no good parts for you. We've got practice, and she's not a morning person even when she gets a good amount of sleep." I hoped this didn't turn into a fight. I'd do it if I had to, but I'd rather just walk her out without trouble.

Ember slid off the guy's lap. "Knight is right. Sorry guys, maybe later." She tried to walk away, but the man who's lap she'd been sitting on grabbed her arm. "What if we're not done?"

"She said no," I hissed.

The guy looked at me, caught sight of the sheer amount of muscle I'd built up in my aerial career with Ember, and backed off.

"Sorry, sorry," he muttered.

Ember walked out next to me, remaining quiet until we were away from the noise of the bar. The warm sand squished between my bare feet and a sea breeze fluttered Ember's hair around her face. She looked out over the water. "What was that all about? We don't have practice for two days."

"I didn't like the way they looked at you," I admitted.

She blinked a few times, then shook her head. "Okay."

"We're going on a tour in the morning, so I wanted to make sure you got some rest."

"We are?"

"Yes."

"Oh, great!" She brightened. "I guess I forgot."

I smiled and put an arm around her, though inside I was trying to figure out what tour we should go on, because I certainly hadn't planned this out. If I was going to die for her, I would just have to make every minute we had together count. Tomorrow I was going to kiss her, and maybe tomorrow evening I'd take her to bed, and if I didn't screw up either of those things too badly, then we'd do it again and again until the princes came to claim my spark and take her away from me.

Dakota Brown

CHAPTER 16

Geraint

Seeing my marks on Ember's neck did something to me I wasn't sure how to describe. It was a possessive feeling that slid through me and gave me ideas about fighting Nic and the other two princes, despite knowing they'd end me with no effort on their part. They'd made me to protect Ember against normal threats, not Nightmare Princes. If I had known what we were going to face on the other side of the mirror, I wouldn't have let Baz's minions take us in the first place. Not that I was certain I could have countered that ray gun they'd pulled, but I would have tried harder. That mistake would haunt me, probably until the moment Nic killed me for marking his princess.

Ember didn't think he was going to keep us apart, but there was no way he would let me continue to be with my spark. Hopefully, she would forgive me for being a little rough with her. I almost never left marks since so much of her body was on display when we performed.

I hoped she forgave me for a lot of things.

I watched her dress in the clothing they'd left. Of course, the beings that had left it were sex demons, so she looked like she was getting ready to perform for an adult show. Not that I was complaining. My fingers itched to remove the things she'd already put on and take her to bed properly this time. Once she finished dressing, she wrinkled her nose in annoyance and shut her eyes. The clothing she wore melded into a more practical set of yoga pants and a long-sleeved t-shirt in muted greens for color. That she had already learned to use some of the land's powers consciously didn't surprise me. She'd always done well at things she put her mind to. The t-shirt didn't hide the bite marks. What had I been thinking? I didn't regret baiting the shadow prince, but I probably would pay for it.

"Are you going to stand there and stare all naked and tempting, or are you going to put some clothing on?"

My dick twitched. Fuck it. They could wait for us.

I grinned and stalked toward her. The worst part of being separated from Ember, besides not knowing if she was okay or not, was not knowing if she would forgive me. Or if I'd be able to hold her again.

Her welcoming expression just made me harder, especially when her clothing melted away as she applied the power to the material. Her pupils dilated with lust, and the flick of her tongue across her lips nearly undid me.

Ember came into my arms just as someone knocked on the door. "Walls aren't that thick, Knight, Spark. We know you're out of the shower. Get out here," Robby shouted.

"Fuck you, Robby," Ember shouted back.

"Leave them alone," I heard Nic say more quietly.

"His highness says to continue to fuck like rabbits, but make it quick. We do have things to sort out," Robby called.

Ember sighed and let her head fall forward.

"Up to you." I ran my hands down her arms.

"This is all so confusing," she admitted.

I folded her into my arms, trying to comfort her. The effort was marginally hindered by my hard dick pressed against her stomach.

She laughed and shifted, rubbing against me.

"It knows what it wants," I said. "And so do I." Though I still expected Nic to come busting through the door, or pop out of a shadow or something, and kick my ass. "I'm sorry, Ember. I'm sorry I couldn't tell you everything. I don't expect you to pick between me and the princes. I'm just glad we're getting more time together before they tell me off."

"If they make me choose, I'll always choose you, Geraint," she whispered. "Regardless of why, you've been there for me most of my life. You're my partner and I trust you more than anyone. I love you, and that's never going to change. I don't care if I'm suddenly dream royalty and you're *only* a knight. You're my knight."

My heart stuttered in my chest at her words. The lump in my throat made it hard to get the rest of the words out, but I pushed them past the emotion. "Spark, Nightmare needs its princess. Maybe now more than ever with the threat it currently faces."

"Nic said he knew a way to dissolve our supposed marriage. We just have to be careful how we do it, so I don't get trapped here." Ember didn't sound happy at the prospect, but she clung to me, shifting back and forth, and rubbing her stomach against my dick. It was getting difficult to think, and I grabbed her ass to make her stop.

She took the opportunity to jump lightly, and I reflexively caught her while she wrapped her legs around my waist.

The grin on her face distracted me further.

"I've missed being in your arms so much, Knight. I can't give you up."

"I don't want to give you up, either, Ember. But I also don't want to see Dream wiped out. Besides, I've seen the way you and Nic look at each other. He's certainly caught your interest."

She sucked her lower lip into her mouth, eyes downcast. "I kissed him. I'm sorry, Geraint. I couldn't figure out how to syphon the shadow essence from him, so we had to be a little more direct. I needed to repair the arch so we could rescue you."

"Spark, it's okay." Surprisingly, the idea of her kissing the shadow prince wasn't bothering me as much as I thought it would.

She raised her beautiful brown eyes and met my gaze. "You're sure?"

"Of course. One, you did what you needed to, to rescue me. Very grateful, by the way." I winked at her. "Two, you are practically married to him. I'm the one who overstepped. Yes, I realize it's your choice, but you also didn't have all the information I did. I don't know how I would have told you, but I probably should have."

My spark took a deep breath. "What do you think I should do?"

She shifted her legs, rubbing the soft fuzz growing where she normally waxed, adding an interesting texture to the motion. I shivered, digging my fingers into her ass. She was leaking all over me and the perfume of her desire just made me harder.

"I think we should make love while we have the chance," I said, voice husky with lust. "Then maybe we should ask Nic what his thoughts are."

"Then get on the bed, Knight."

"Yes, your highness," I murmured and did as instructed.

"On your back," she ordered. "You have a little apologizing to do."

The wicked grin curling her perfect lips and the amused light in her eye gave me an idea of what she wanted.

I set her on the edge of the bed, then crawled all the way on and lay down. Ember walked on her knees until she was next to me. Then she stood and straddled me.

"Better make it a good one," she said as she slid down into a split, right over my face.

"Anything for you, Spark." I grabbed her hips and flicked my tongue across her soaked lips.

Her urgent moan of pleasure spurred me on, and I put my tongue to work, years of practice guiding me as I worked to bring the woman I loved as much pleasure as I could. I wished we had all night, but I also knew I was lucky enough to have even a short time together.

Ember trembled, and I tightened my grip on her as her muscles tightened. Her breathing quickened.

"Just like that," she whispered. I could imagine her eyes closed and her head thrown back in ecstasy, mouth slightly parted as she breathed my name, as her body shattered while I sucked her clit.

She shuddered, gasping, and her juices flooded out of her, coating my face.

I wouldn't get the smell out of my beard for days, and that was okay with me.

Ember curled out of her splits and lay next to me. It wasn't the most practical position for her to sit on my face, but she enjoyed the challenge of holding the pose while coming all over my face. I certainly wasn't going to complain.

"Ready?" I asked.

"Yes, my love." She twisted onto her back.

I positioned myself above her, pushing one of her legs back against her chest, taking advantage of her flexibility and practically folding her in half. She loved how deep I could go like this.

Caging myself inside my Spark was no trouble. She was so wet, so slick, so full of desire for me. I plunged as

193

deeply inside her as I could, her inner walls tightening around me. She whimpered in reaction.

Normally, she would have been crying out as loudly as she liked, but I suspected she kept it down because of Nic and Robby in the other room. Part of me wanted her to scream with pleasure, but the other part of me knew I was pushing Nic pretty far as it was.

Her quiet cries of pleasure as I thrust into her and the expression of love in her eyes as she met my eyes nearly undid me before I was ready. I wanted her to come on my cock though, and I wasn't going to finish until she did.

I pressed my hand down on her lower stomach and rubbed her clit with thumb.

"Geraint!" she cried urgently, trembling as she met my thrusts with her own.

"Just tell me when, Spark."

"Now, oh please, now!"

One final flick of my thumb, a quick thrust and she sailed over the edge, inner walls clamping down on me and pulling me along with her.

I released the leg I'd had trapped against her chest, and rolled us to our sides so we could cuddle.

We didn't speak, just held each other until our bodies calmed down enough that I could slide out of her without it being too much stimulation.

She grinned at me. "I think we need another shower."

"A quick one, Spark. We're testing their patience as it is."

"Aww," she pouted. "But shower sex after bed sex is my favorite."

I laughed. "We already had shower sex."

"That was angry sex. I want happy shower sex." She pushed her lip out.

Unable to resist, I kissed her, sucking her lip into my mouth.

"Maybe, if you're really good." I gave in.

She sprang to her feet and dashed for the bathroom, only wobbling a little from the endorphins flooding her system.

Hoping this wasn't my last time with Ember, I chased her into the bathroom.

CHAPTER 17

Ember

While everything wasn't completely right in my world, I felt a hell of a lot better after enough orgasms that I'd lost count while reconnecting with my Knight. I was also sore, but I'd take it.

We dressed, and I helped Geraint change his clothing into something a little more his style. Jeans and a t-shirt would be fine for whatever we had planned. I could always adjust it later if it turned out we needed specialized clothing. If nothing else, I was really enjoying my ability to control the shadow essence.

I couldn't help the sheepish smile as Geraint and I finally left the bedroom. Nic and Robby sat in the main room, waiting. Nic's eyes narrowed when he saw the bruises Geraint had left on my neck, and he faded into shadow for a few seconds before solidifying again.

My knight twitched next to me, but didn't say anything.

Robby smirked at me. Or maybe he was smirking at Geraint. Either way, Nic was obviously trying to ignore what we'd been up to.

"You two are completely ridiculous," Robby said. "I swear, we can't take you anywhere. Do you remember the time you almost missed a curtain call because someone couldn't keep his dick out of your—"

Nic cleared his throat. "Jester, shut up."

"Why?" Robby crossed his arms. "We need to sort out your little problem before it becomes a big problem."

Nic laughed. "The knight doesn't need to worry about me. I accept that it's Ember's right to choose her lovers. It's Dio you need to be wary of. He'll kill you for this. He's seen Ember as ours since before we played our silly children's game."

"Is that your plan, then?" I snapped. "Wait for Dio to solve your problem for you?"

Nic shrugged. "That's one way to handle the situation."

I was about to rage at Nic, but taking the easy path is probably what I would have done in his place, too. *Damn it.*

"Do you, or do you not, want your princess?" Robby pushed.

Nic clenched his jaw. "It's not my decision," he finally said.

"Nice non-answer." Robby steepled his fingers.

"It's far more important for us to figure out what we need to do about Baz and the nothingness, than if I want to fuck Ember," Nic bit out.

"Have you considered that the problems might be related?" Robby said.

I dragged Geraint the rest of the way into the room, and we sank down onto the couch. He sat stiffly, but I leaned against him. Nic stared at the floor.

"I do not think sex will solve our problems," the prince replied.

"It might." Robby shrugged. "But if you're not going to talk about it, fine. What are you planning to do with Baz, and where is Dio?"

"Baz I'm going to kill. Screw the consequences," Nic said. "I have no idea where Dio is."

"Hmm, perhaps we need to find our primal prince. You might need help with Baz, after all. Especially if you aren't going to claim your princess."

"What does Ember have to do with it?" Nic sighed, as if conceding a point to the jester.

"Your powers, and her powers, will increase the more you share energy. That's nearly the entire point of having a mortal partner, bringing human imagination in to refresh Dream and Nightmare." Robby got up, clasped his hands behind his back, and paced on the other side of the room from us. "Baz won't go down easily."

Nic shrugged. "Then he'll kill me, and maybe it'll trigger a reset in the process."

"A reset?" I asked. "You mentioned something about that before."

"It's the way new Dream and Nightmare princes and princesses are born, if you will. The energy comes together to create new ones. Usually it's because the old ones have lost relevance to humanity."

"So, there isn't always a prince of shadows?"

"No. Fortunately, Baz, Dio, and I were formed of powerful fears that have remained relevant for most of humanity."

"Well, cool, I guess."

Geraint straightened. "Ember, did you remember to tell Prince Nic that Baz didn't recognize you at all?"

"Yeah, of course I—shit. I was going to, but I got distracted, and then I forgot."

"Baz did not recognize you at all?" Nic leaned forward.

"No. He had no idea I was the aerialist he was looking for."

"Your highness," Geraint said. "I honestly think if I hadn't been with her, he wouldn't have figured it out at all."

"Yeah, and I guess along those same lines, I recognized I knew you somehow, even before the block on my memories faded away. I still have no sense of familiarity with Baz." I threaded my fingers together to keep from fidgeting. "You said he should have been able to sense us when we were sneaking around the castle. What happened?"

Nic and Robby stared at each other, seeming to have a silent conversation.

"Well, this is very interesting." Robby finally broke eye contact. "Perhaps not only do we need to find Dio, but we need to find the real Baz, too."

"What do you mean?" Geraint asked.

"It is entirely possible that the man who has been parading around as Prince Baz for the last however many years is some sort of changeling. If so, the real Baz must be alive, or you likely would have noticed his demise." Robby resumed pacing.

"That would explain a lot. I can sense his presence, but it's not the same as it used to be," Nic said. "Now I really wish I had slit his throat."

"What do we do?" I glanced at Geraint. His brow furrowed as he thought.

"What we do is find The Lady in White and get you home," Nic said. "I'm keeping the jester with me, but you and your knight don't need to be involved with the search for either Dio or Baz. It's too dangerous, and I can move faster on my own."

I couldn't argue with that, though I wanted to.

"Mmm, if you completed your bond with your princess, she could step through shadows just like you," Robby suggested.

"You don't know that," Nic snapped.

"The possibility is very high."

"She is not mine." Nic glared at Robby. "And you need to stop suggesting otherwise."

I noticed that not once had he said he didn't want me. That twisted me up inside. I had Geraint. He was more than enough. He was perfect. *Why do I want to go comfort Nic now?*

Robby spread his hands in front of him. "Very well. Then we focus on The Lady and get Ember and Geraint home where they can go on with their lives. Though it appears you'll have to search for a new manager." He bowed sardonically. "My apologies."

I didn't even want to think about that right now.

As if waiting for us to come to that conclusion, someone knocked on the door. The timing had to be coincidence, but then again, this was Dream. Maybe it wasn't.

Robby got the door and let a woman into the room. She looked like she was ready for a trek through the jungle, except her shirt was too tight, buttons about to burst, her shorts were way too short, and her boots just a bit too sexy for an actual hike.

"I'm Camila," she purred. "I'll be your guide. What is it you seek?" She bowed to Nic, a deep plunge toward the floor that showed off her perfectly shaped ass.

It would have been ridiculous, but she made it the sexiest bow I'd ever seen. "Freaking sex demons," I muttered.

Geraint chuckled and kissed my head.

"We seek the Lady in White," Nic answered the succubus.

"When would you like to leave?" Camila straightened and simpered at Nic.

"It occurs to me we've been traveling for hours. We started yesterday in the conscious realm, and the humans need to be fed. Rest is warranted," Robby said.

"Agreed." Nic shot Robby an annoyed look. "We can leave in twelve hours once we've rested and eaten."

Camila nodded. "A good plan. I will have food sent up. While I wait, I will make inquiries as to the Lady's whereabouts."

"Carefully," Nic cautioned. "We don't want her harmed."

"Yes, of course, your highness." She bowed again, then left the room.

The creeping exhaustion that had plagued me all day was back, along with a fierce hunger that I hadn't noticed until Robby had mentioned it.

"Sleep would probably be good." I yawned. "Are we safe here?"

"We should be," Nic said.

"Good." I snuggled into Geraint's arms and tried not to notice the pained expression on Nic's face. Robby was right. We probably needed to talk some of this out. But did it really matter if I was going home? Nic didn't seem to think he needed my help, and I was just as happy to leave him to whatever he had planned.

My eyes fluttered shut while I was wrestling with my thoughts. I was vaguely aware of Geraint cradling me in his arms and carrying me to bed, but after that I was out.

***

The ambient light hadn't changed since the last time we had stepped outside. It was still just dark enough for Nic to be comfortable, but bright enough for us to see reasonably well and not have to squint. Succubi and incubi wandered around the town looking just like the sexy demons they were. I tried not to get too interested in the eye-candy, remembering what had happened when I'd focused on the clouds in Nightmare.

Camila set out, and we followed, back to the road we'd traveled the day before.

"I found the barest hint of a rumor as to the mirror dweller's location," Camila said. "We head for the cliffs."

"The cliffs?"

"Another boundary feature," Robby explained. "Some people absolutely love climbing and leaping from heights, others have nothing but nightmares about it. The cliffs dwell in the boundaries."

"Oh, great. So, we're climbing?" I twisted my hands together.

"It appears so," Robby said.

I didn't reply. Would I even be able to climb? Once upon a time a few weeks ago, I would have managed just fine. Especially if we could manifest some silks. Then it was easy enough to rest on the way up. Now? I hadn't conquered my fears yet, and it sounded like I might have to face them head on. The thought did not excite me.

"Are we walking the entire way?" Robby sounded displeased by the idea.

"The wolves are busy," Nic grumbled.

"Very well. I'll see what I can do. One moment." He turned sideways and vanished.

"What the hell!" I spun around, looking for my friend. I knew he had some sort of ability to hide like Nic did, but I'd not seen him simply vanish into thin air like that.

"He must be feeling better," Nic said.

"Did he need to recover from being gone?" I asked.

The shadow prince nodded.

Camila, unfazed, continued on down the road.

"And you and he could just, like, teleport there or something?" I walked next to the prince.

He shifted a touch closer to me, probably unconsciously. The edges of the shadow that followed him everywhere brushed against my arm. I didn't pull away.

"Yes, but that would separate us until you caught up. I'd rather know you are safe."

"Why don't you just go look and see if she's there, and then return," I suggested.

"I had considered that option, but I don't want to draw attention to her more than we have to. Two visits might get noticed where one might not."

"Oh."

"We aren't in a hurry," Nic said. "We shouldn't tarry, but the world isn't going to end just because we took an extra day in the boundary lands."

"Okay." I stayed at his side and Geraint followed while Camila led.

Nic's presence brushed against my awareness, just like the edges of his shadow stroked the back of my hand and my forearm. Unlike the cold, clingy shadow stuff that I'd experienced in Nightmare Castle, Nic's shadowy self felt warm and softly caressed my skin.

Feeling conflicted, I let my mind wander while we walked. Robby said Nightmare needed its princess. Only I could wield the energy to repair the arches and I did think they needed fixing, but without the mirror dwellers, was there any point? And couldn't I just fix them and then go home?

I wasn't ready to be tied down with responsibility. I didn't want to have to confront hard questions and push for answers. Isn't that what being a princess was? Responsibility? I imagined even here that translated. It wasn't like I wasn't responsible. We fulfilled our contracts, showed up on time, put our all into every performance, but that was the life I wanted. Not the life of a princess in a land I didn't even know was real.

Nic grabbed my hand and pulled me to a halt before I blundered into Camila's back. The shadow essence surged between us at the contact, flowing into me. I thought I felt some of my energy transfer back to Nic. He sucked in a breath, clearly not prepared for that. Not that I had been. I trembled, an aching need settling into me. I should have been satisfied from earlier, but something coiled deep inside, longing for more.

"Nightmare needs its princess," Robby said softly, riding up on a white horse.

I gasped, the beautiful animal distracting me a little from my desire to climb Nic like a tree.

Three additional white horses followed. They didn't have horns, but they had silver hooves that rang like quiet bells even on the dirt path. None wore saddles, but I suspected we didn't need any.

Nic hadn't let go of my hand, his fingers tight on mine, a slight tremor noticeable in his grip. Actually, that might have been me. I couldn't pull away. It wasn't just the magic of the game we'd played binding us together. I really did like Nic. The prince had helped rescue Geraint when he didn't have to. He cared about his people. And Nic was a fantastic kisser. All of my memories from our time together as children didn't hurt either. I'd loved all three of them in my childhood way.

Geraint didn't say anything, but his presence behind me was palpable. Was there a way through this? I remembered what Robby had said when they thought I wasn't able to hear, that thing about the princes all expecting to share me and what was one more. *Was that a solution?*

I didn't know, and I wasn't brave enough to ask. Maybe that was what I wanted, but I had no idea how it could possibly work out. My vision got a little wavy while I stood there, frozen.

Geraint put his hands on my shoulders and leaned forward. "Breathe, Spark."

Startled out of whatever daze I'd been in, I jerked, sucking in a breath. My vision cleared, and I pulled my hand from Nic's. That seemed to release him from a similar trance. He tucked his hands into his sleeves. Or was that a cloak? Or shadows. His clothing shifted and the features he didn't keep a tight hold on, like the length of his hair, blurred.

Robby seemed to stare at me, but when I looked closer, I thought he was staring at Geraint, instead. My knight's fingers tightened on my shoulders, and he kissed my cheek before stepping away.

"My apologies," Nic said, and hurried out of reach.

I rubbed my arms and tried not to feel cold without his hand on mine. The essence I'd absorbed from Nic still coiled inside me as if content to replace what I'd given Nic.

"Grab a horse, Princess," Robby ordered. "This will be much swifter."

Not completely free of the daze that had settled over me, I approached one of the horses and held out my hand.

She nickered, whiskers tickling my hand as she touched me with her muzzle.

"Let me give you a leg up," Geraint said, coming over behind me.

The heat from my knight's chest warmed my back, and I took a step backward until I was pressed against him.

"What do I do?" I whispered sadly.

"Right now, we concentrate on getting home," he said. "Then we figure out the rest."

Nodding because I couldn't speak for the damn lump in my throat, I let Geraint help me on the horse. I gave her a pat and wrapped my fingers in her mane. Though I didn't regret the short marathon sex with my knight, I was a little sore and sitting on the back of a horse made me acutely aware of it.

She whickered and once Geraint was mounted, the horses moved off. Camila rode easily and sexily. I would have been amused if I hadn't had so many other worries on my mind. Nic had no issues with the horse, but Geraint and I probably looked out of place on the backs of our forgiving mounts. At least we had years of aerial and gymnastics to help our balance and athleticism. That had to count for a lot.

When the horses increased their pace, I squeaked in alarm but held on. I felt bad for my horse, but she kept her ears forward. I hoped that meant I wasn't doing too badly.

Our tireless mounts cantered along the dirt track, the soft chime of their hooves like music I wanted to dance to. I wondered what sort of dream had spawned these horses.

Could I learn to love it here? This insane land of menacing clouds and friendly wolves? Maybe. Did I want to stay? Maybe I could visit sometime? But, if I weren't the princess, I'd be dreambound, and I'd never leave.

The luxury to come and go wasn't one everyone had access to. But if I wasn't going to be the princess, I had no right to hang on to the title and the freedom, not to mention my hold on the shadow prince.

The thought of giving up Nic hurt more than it should have. We had history together. Childhood games and summers spent running wild in the forest. Was that enough?

I glanced at Geraint, riding next to me, and wondered if any of my thoughts were obvious. He looked troubled, which was such a foreign expression on his usually carefree face. I wanted to soothe the wrinkles from his brow and kiss the worry from his down-turned lips.

Yet I also wanted to massage the tension from Nic's shoulders and fold myself into his arms so he could keep me safe from the nightmares that lurked in the darkness. Resolving those two conflicting desires was beyond me, at least currently. The simple route was to go home and put this behind me. That was the path we were on, and deviating from it involved danger I couldn't even fathom. I'd stay on the easy road. The road that left me in Geraint's arms, and without the responsibilities of caring for a land I didn't even understand.

Feeling guilty, I tried to focus on the beauty of the strange land around me. For a moment I was excited about the chance to see Dream soon, then remembered we were going back to the conscious realm. I likely wouldn't see Dream ever.

I clenched my jaw and tried to corral my unruly thoughts.

They refused to be ignored, but finally the horses slowed. We'd come to the cliffs, and we were most certainly going to be climbing.

The horses halted. I stared up at the ledges high in the air above us and my hands shook. Surely, Nic could use his shadowy power to sweep me up the cliffs in no time. Right? Was it even fair to ask him to carry me? And what about Geraint? As civil as Nic was being about my knight, I doubted he wanted to haul Geraint up a rock face. Could Robby?

The ledges jutted out over the road, casting dim shadows that blended in with the surroundings, obscuring the edges of the darkness. The flat tans and whites of the bare rock contrasted with the green forest we'd just ridden through. I was getting used to the lack of shades in the color palate here, but it still caught me off guard every time the landscape changed.

"How do we get up?"

"Since you will not take the easier route," Robby said. "You and Knight will have to climb. Perhaps I should scout ahead, anyway. If The Lady isn't there, we have no reason to scale the cliffs."

"Your highness, we need to get off the road," Camila said. "We'll find her farther in."

Nic studied the succubus before nodding. "Very well."

It might have been my imagination, but the idea of leaving the road seemed to make Nic a little nervous.

"This way."

We followed our sexy guide from the dirt path and onto a narrow stone trail. The horses' hooves rang and echoed around us as we wound through this world's equivalent of a slot canyon.

I was relaxing into my mount's easy gate, rocking my hips with her motion and loosening my back. The scenery was beautiful, and I looked around while we rode.

A quick darting motion caught my attention. I twisted to look behind me. Geraint stared off to the side.

"What are those?"

Something scampered up the rock wall.

"Probably lizards of some sort or another," Camila replied, sounding unconcerned. "Maybe some dinosaurs."

"Should we be worried?" Geraint asked.

"No. Keep an eye on them, but overall, we're in no danger from the wildlife." Camila patted her horse. "Watch our mounts," she continued. "If they get upset, then we'll worry."

"Okay." I had to trust her. That didn't stop me from glancing at Nic.

He kept his gaze moving around, but didn't seem overly bothered.

I glanced back at my knight, who shrugged. He knew only marginally more about this land than I did.

Before we could move off, the horses threw up their heads and snorted. I had only moments to worry about what was going on before they bolted. Nic rode up next to me, wrapping shadows around my waist to hold me to the

209

horse. Something dove around us, and red streaked across the horse's flank in front of me. It kicked out and ran faster.

More creatures dove around us, sharp wings slicing at my arm.

"Birds," Nic said. "Corvids. You can trace that fear back to a movie."

Geraint and Nic did their best to hold off the rain of black birds trying to slice us with wings and beaks. Nic with his shadows and Geraint with a sword he'd pulled from somewhere. Nic's shadows provided us a shield, but it wasn't perfect, and we were still cut and bleeding by the time the horses slowed.

"There." Camila pointed up.

"Jester," Nic ordered.

Robby gave Nic a sardonic bow from horseback before sliding off, turning sideways, and disappearing.

The birds continued to pelt us around Nic's shadows. He shoved out a burst of essence and pushed the birds away.

"It won't last, but that will give us a minute or two."

We didn't have to wait long before Robby reappeared. "She's there and willing to help."

"Camila, all my thanks," Nic said to the succubus.

"Of course, your highness. Anything I can do for you will be my pleasure." Her tone of voice made it obvious she was open to the possibilities. I tried not to let it bother me.

I looked up again. It was only twenty or thirty feet in the air. I could do it. Really. I'd almost rather face the birds.

"I will take you," Nic said. "We don't have much time."

I hadn't noticed him come over next to me. He put his hand over mine, smoothing some of the tension away with his touch. This time, our contact wasn't as intense, but the desire deep inside me perked up and took notice.

"If we fashion fabric to climb like you are used to, knight, can you ascend on your own?"

"Yes," Geraint said. "Ember shouldn't have any issues, either." He shot me a puzzled look, and it occurred to me he hadn't experienced my reaction to Baz's torture yet.

"Heights and I aren't getting along very well right now," I admitted, casting my gaze toward the ground and trying to ignore the shame that caught in my throat like a lump.

"None of that," Nic said. "It's not your fault, and you'll get through it. Now is simply not the time to confront your very justifiable fear."

I nodded.

"Ahh, right," Geraint replied with understanding. "Yeah, we'll work on it back in the conscious realm."

Nic waved his hand and a set of black silks tumbled from the edge of the cliff, unfurling. For a minute my fingers itched to climb, to perform, and then the fear came crashing back and I looked away.

Geraint didn't waste time, wrapping his hands around the fabric, trapping it between his feet, and climbing swiftly toward the ledge.

Robby again vanished after stroking the lead horse on the shoulder. I gave mine a quick pat. Nic put his hands on my hips. Automatically, I put my hands on his shoulders for support, and he helped me slide off into his arms.

My heart raced, and my breath caught, and my desire surged. Nic held me tightly, and I folded myself into his arms.

"I'm sorry," I whispered.

"For what, luv?"

"For all of this. For that stupid game, for things being difficult between us, for putting your people in danger."

Nic tightened his arms around me and kissed my temple. "We all wanted to play your game, Ember. It's okay. None of us knew. None of that is your fault."

Sighing, I rested my head on his shoulder. "What will you do?"

"Get you and the knight home and relatively safe. He can guard you as he always has. The rest... Well, I want to say it's none of your concern, but that would be unfair. As I said, try to find Dio, try to stop Baz. I guess attempt to locate the real Baz if this one is indeed an imposter. Once things are settled, we will find you and release you from your bonds to our land. You can keep Geraint, of course."

I nodded, unable to speak. It was a fair plan, but I didn't like it. It seemed ridiculous and perhaps even cruel to argue, however.

"Let's get this over with." Nic lowered his hands until he cupped my ass. "Put your legs around my waist so I can carry you like before."

"Easier to jump with your hands on my waist."

He chuckled, kneading my butt. "I believe the current saying is 'my bad.'"

I snorted, put my hands back on his shoulders, and jumped lightly. He lifted, and I wrapped my thighs around him. Nic shrouded us in shadow, and like before, when he'd rescued me from my fear, I didn't feel the transition as he climbed. Probably it had to do with his magic, keeping me from freaking out or something. I trusted him, but I also appreciated the effort.

"We're there," he whispered, one hand going to the small of my back, supporting me.

I unburied my face from his shoulder and slowly unwrapped my legs from his waist. "Thank you, Nic."

"Of course, Ember."

Avoiding Geraint's eyes, I moved farther from the edge. Robby motioned, and we all headed toward a cave in the cliff face. The narrow gash in the stone opened into a cave that had to be operating on dream logic. There was no way the immense cavern would have fit into the space I saw outside. Also, it was lit with globes of floating light. I loved it, but certainly dream logic.

An unshattered mirror circled in a gilt frame was mounted to the stone, and Robby stood next to it.

We went over to join him.

The woman that looked back at us swayed as if caught in an unseen wind. Her white skirts billowed, and the shawl she wore flapped dramatically. Her long blond hair floated almost as if she were underwater. Unlike Mary, she didn't appear completely terrifying at first sight. Her porcelain skin stretched tightly over high cheekbones and looked papery thin. She had a prominent nose and piercing blue eyes. The only color to her was her eyes and her hair. Clearly a ghost, or, in this case, a mirror dweller.

"Lady," I said respectfully.

"Princess." The sadness in her voice broke my heart, and I clutched at my chest. Most of the ghost stories I remembered involving any lady in white were unhappy ones.

Nic bowed to the mirror. "You will assist these two in returning to the conscious realm?"

"She can repair the arch?"

"Yes," Nic confirmed.

"Then I will take them. Once it is done, this sanctuary will be discovered. I will hide in another and hope I am not found."

"We are deeply indebted to you for this service," Nic said. "We are working to resolve the conflict instead of merely trying to survive as we once were."

"The princess will return and fight?"

"Ember has tasks she must accomplish in the conscious realm."

The Lady in White eyed Nic as if she sensed his deception, but still she nodded her agreement. "Then let us be away before we are discovered."

Nic touched my arm, and I turned to face him.

"Be careful, luv." He kissed my forehead and stepped away.

"Spark, if you so much as break a nail, I'm taking it out on Knight, so be careful." Robby wrapped me in a hug before giving Geraint a quicker one.

"Knight, take care of her," Nic ordered before turning away.

Geraint laced his fingers through mine. I put my free hand on the mirror. I held more of the shadow essence than I'd ever managed before and it only used a small amount to repair the connections so The Lady could open the way for us.

The cool liquid feel of sinking into the mirror flowed over my hand and up my arm, and then we were stepping into the mirror in a much calmer transition than I'd yet experienced. The archway The Lady had opened for us looked to be a lane of flowering trees with pink blooms and branches that touched overhead, making a tunnel. It stretched into the distance ahead of us and I could almost imagine I smelled the blossoms. Much more cheerful than the stone arches Bloody Mary created. I wondered if each mirror dweller had a distinct style of arch.

I supposed I'd never know.

We stepped out of the cabin mirror. I inhaled a breath of home, dusty, a hint of mold, and the fragrant scent of the forest. My eyes feasted on the multitude of colors present even in the falling-down log cabin. The humidity brought sweat to my brow, and I sneezed. It felt so good to be home.

I turned. "Thank you, Lady."

"Princess," she replied. "If you mean to remain in the conscious realm, so be it. But we need someone to take your place. Dream is being consumed, and I do not know if it will survive without our mortal royalty. It is long past time for the Dream princesses to find their match, and the Nightmare princes need theirs to become whole again."

I nodded. What did you say when someone told you the very survival of a realm depended on you?

She faded out before I could come up with something better. I knew I was supposed to break the arch behind me, but The Lady had left it, and I couldn't bring myself to sever the connection.

Geraint said nothing about my omission, just took my hand and tugged gently. "Let's get home, Ember. We've got a lot to figure out, and I'm sure your parents want to know you're safe."

"They want to know you're safe, too, Geraint. They love you as if you were their own."

"Did anyone happen to mention to them I wasn't from around here?" A hint of mischief twinkled in his eyes.

"Yeah, they know. I don't think they cared."

"They've always been so accepting. I'm glad they practically adopted me."

"Yeah, but not actually, otherwise you and I would be even more awkward of a couple."

He burst out laughing. "True, Spark. Very true."

CHAPTER 18

Ember

Memories

"Honey, come down here!"

"Just a second, Mom!" I shouted from the top of the silks. I was almost done setting up the drop.

I glanced down at my instructor, and she nodded that I had it right, so I let myself fall backward, spinning down, stopping my spiral with my legs, then flipping back upright to end in a pose.

"Point your toes!" Clara reminded me.

"Thank you," I said for the reminder and pointed my toes.

"Don't forget to stretch out, Ember," Clara said as I scampered over to see what Mom wanted.

"I won't!"

A boy about my age stood next to Mom. He had blond hair, stormy gray eyes, and a hesitant smile on his face.

"Hi!" I said when I ran up to him.

"Hello." He waived hesitantly.

"Your accent is amazing. I'm Ember."

"Geraint," he replied shyly.

I tried out the name a few times before I got it right. At his nod, I grinned. "Great! Are you staying with us for the summer?"

"Yes. Your parents were kind enough to squeeze me in to the summer camp."

I knew that meant he was one of the foster kids that came to our summer programs. It got them out, doing fun things, and in return for their stay, they helped around the place. Not much. Mostly just with things like dishes after meals, some of the gardening, and cleaning the gym. Easy stuff. Anything complicated the adults handled.

"I'm glad you're here. I'll show you around."

Geraint glanced up at Mom. She nodded and shooed us away. "Stretch, Ember," she called after me.

"Yes, Mom." I ran over to a mat. "I can show you one of our cool down routines first. And then I'll give you the tour. Are you going to be an aerialist, too?"

"I would like that, I think," Geraint answered.

"I'm going to be a famous performer," I said. "I'll travel the world and do silks acts and everyone will love me. Maybe you can be my partner." I grinned at him.

Geraint, who had joined me while I stretched, grinned back. "I'd like that very much."

CHAPTER 19

Ember

"You can do it, Spark," Ash called.

I'd made it halfway up the silks this time before my limbs trembled and my hands refused to budge. It had taken me a week to get this far. I was making progress, just more slowly than I'd like.

Geraint had the rolling scaffold nearby in case he had to rescue me. So far, he'd only had to do it once, but knowing he was there helped.

Mom taught a group of kids in one corner of the gym, and Casey taught a handful of teens how to use the lyra. She'd decided to spend the summer with us, after all. No one had told her about my adventures in Nightmare. Which was just as well. Explaining that… Well, I didn't think I could. She hadn't asked why I was freaking out about heights, for which I was grateful. I wondered if she ever would, and if she did, what I would say.

"Up or down, Spark," Geraint urged. "You've got this."

His Irish lilt soothed me, and I took a breath and nodded.

"Up," I said, not loud enough for anyone else to hear, but I was going up. Pretend Baz would no longer have a hold on me. I just needed to make it to the top.

I pushed my feet out, sliding my hands up the silks before gripping, unwrapping my feet and pulling my knees to my chest. I did one of the easiest climbs. No need to make it complicated. I just had to get to the top. Re-wrapping my feet took only a moment, and then I straightened. Higher. I went higher than I'd been since Baz had dropped me. The silks were still there. This wasn't a nightmare, and if it were, I could control it. At least for a while longer, I was a princess of Nightmare, and the shadow essence obeyed my command.

Higher.

My forearms burned, tired from the attempts I'd made already today. I almost didn't notice that I'd reached the top until I ran out of fabric to grab.

Ash whooped.

It felt silly to be so excited about something that, for me, was incredibly simple, but I felt good making it to the top.

I hung for a moment before wrapping my leg around the silk, trapping it between my feet and sliding to the ground. No need to make it fancy.

Geraint wrapped me in a tight hug. "Good job, Spark."

"Thank you. We'll be back in the air together in no time."

"I want nothing more," he replied.

That brought to mind another conversation I'd been avoiding. Maybe I could have it now that I'd at least sort of conquered one of my fears.

"You two go have some celebratory, uh, fun, or something," Ash said, looking over her shoulder to see how close the kids were.

"Thanks, Ash." I wrapped my cousin in a big hug, then glanced at my knight. He nodded, so we headed for the house.

"Do you really want to keep performing with me?"

"Yes, Ember, of course I do." He took my hand.

"But, really. I mean, what else would you rather be doing?"

Geraint stopped me and made me face him. "Spark, I want nothing more than to be at your side. Whatever the reason, this is what I want. I may not have chosen to be created to guard you, nor did I choose my initial path on this world, but I've never regretted it. I did choose to allow you into my heart and into my bed, even knowing it could cost me my life. I just couldn't watch you with anyone else. I chose us, Ember. I love you. For real. I wasn't created to love you. I was only created to keep you safe. Everything else was my decision."

"You're sure?"

"Yes, Spark. I'm sure. I'm also sure we both stink. Let's go shower. It's close to dinnertime." He put his arm around me, and we went inside.

I thought I heard tapping when we went through the den, but I must have been imagining things because I didn't see anything when I looked around. Maybe it was from the kitchen?

"I guess I can see why you didn't want to get married," I said once we were in our room. I shed my clothing and my knight did the same. He was right. We smelled like we'd been in the gym for hours.

"Yeah, you're essentially already married."

"Thanks for the reminder," I muttered. "What are we going to do about that?"

"Nothing to be done until Nic shows up with the other princes."

I nodded.

"You don't like the idea of giving them up, do you?"

"What else can I do?"

Geraint pulled me back against his chest, and I rested my cheek on his shoulder.

"There are lots of options, Ember."

"They all involve either giving you up, or giving Nic up. Baz and Dio were great friends, but I haven't seen them in years. I don't even know if I still like them."

He squeezed me. "I think you probably will."

"But...three husbands? And where does that leave you?"

Geraint took a deep breath. "I don't know. What do you want? Ideal scenario?"

"I've always been a fan of having cake and getting to eat it, but I don't see how that's fair to anyone. We just have to find someone to take my place. Maybe Ash will do it."

"I was under the impression that Ash didn't prefer men."

"Right, but I bet she'd make a fantastic princess. She's a lawyer, smart, loves taking care of people, she's perfect. Except for the not-liking-guys thing. There's probably a way around that. Besides, she's got a future wifey. Maybe they can both be princesses."

"What if you could have all four of us?"

"That's a lot of cocks." I blurted out the first thing that came to my mind.

Geraint laughed and turned on the shower. "I imagine there are worse things."

"Yeah, like not enough cocks," I replied. "Are you serious?"

He shrugged. "Something to consider. I know you like Nic. He likes you. I'm not willing to give you up, but Nic, at least, might consider the idea."

"I think Robby said something along those same lines to Nic. I didn't hear what his reply was."

"I never expected to get to keep you once the princes came for you, but I also expected them to come much sooner than they did. If I'd have known then what I know now, I'd have given in to you much sooner. Also, I never would have let them take us a few weeks ago. I regret that."

"Now we know. Also, they had guns."

He nodded.

The water had warmed, and we got busy cleaning up. We were just about to get busy in other ways when someone screamed from the den.

"What the hell?"

We rushed out of the shower. I dried off just enough to not be drenched and pulled on the dream clothing I still had and formed it into a workout outfit.

Geraint struggled into a pair of sweats, and we ran out into the den.

Two kids huddled on the floor, sobbing, while an older teen comforted them.

"Monster in the mirror," one of them gasped out, pointing.

I looked into the mirror over the fireplace. Bloody Mary appeared looking worse than normal, skin torn, leaking fluid, and showing bone. She gestured wildly and mouthed "cabin."

Geraint and I rushed out the door, sprinting for the woods. Neither of us had extra breath for conversation, and my sides heaved by the time we made it. I clutched at the door handle, sucking in air. Geraint shoved on the door after I jiggled the knob, and we went inside.

"Princess," Mary called from the cabin mirror. She sounded muted and far away, though her battered image was right there. "It's Nic. He needs you."

"What do I do?"

223

"Just take him from me." Mary looked over her shoulder, eyes wide.

I reached into the mirror and felt familiar hands grab weakly at mine. A shadowy form appeared in the depths of the mirror, and I yanked.

Mary screamed in pain. Geraint grabbed me around the waist and pulled, and I refused to let go of Nic. We tumbled backward, dragging the Nightmare prince out of the mirror. He landed on top of me, feeling way lighter than he should, nearly insubstantial, as if he truly were a shadow of himself.

The mirror fractured, glass splitting loudly, almost covering the sound of Mary's agonized screams as whatever had been after her caught up to her.

Geraint helped me untangle myself from him and Nic.

"He looks like he was drained," I gasped, hand covering my mouth. Nic looked like a black and white drawing, no color left, flat, almost lifeless. Even the shadow that usually shifted around him was still. His hair, normally in a ponytail, was free, and I brushed some of it out of his face.

"You still carry essence, right?"

"Yeah."

"Give it to Nic. As much as you can. He's dying," Geraint said urgently.

"Okay." I leaned over and pressed my lips to Nic's. He was cold and unresponsive, but it gave me a connection to pass the essence to him.

He took it all, and slowly, life returned to his features. His chest rose weakly, and he coughed. I helped him roll on his side.

"Nic," I cried out.

"Ember?"

I pulled the Nightmare prince into my lap and held him while he recovered. "Are you okay?" It was a dumb question. Obviously, he wasn't.

"I think I will recover," he answered after an extended silence, voice labored.

"What do you need?"

"Rest," he said, weakly. "And you."

I shivered and glanced up at Geraint. He nodded.

Geraint and I helped Nic to his feet, arms draped over our shoulders. He at least looked human at the moment. Though, that actually wasn't a good thing, because he typically didn't look human unless he was trying.

My stomach twisted with worry as we helped the Nightmare prince stumble from the cabin and through the forest.

Nic spent all his energy walking, breath rasping harshly.

We hesitated at the edge of the forest. The sun beat down, raising a humid haze over the gardens. Sweat ran along my spine and beaded on my brow. The shower I'd taken earlier was basically useless at this point. Nic had felt light when he'd landed on me, but dragging him through the forest had let me know exactly how tall and heavy he really was. Nic was taller than Geraint and had a good six inches on me.

"I don't think we can keep you out of the sun," I said. "Do you want me to run and get a blanket?"

"No," Nic rasped. "It'll be okay. Just get me inside."

He flinched when we stepped from the shade. Geraint and I picked up our pace as much as we could, and Nic stumbled along with us. The sunlight faded out what color he'd regained in his skin, and he sagged in our grip.

"Spark!" Ash yelled.

We kept going. "It's Nic. Get the door? Clear the den?"

225

She raced ahead. I loved my cousin so much.

By the time we made it to the house, no one occupied the living area. Ash held the door and shut it behind us.

Nic sighed in relief once we were out of the sun. The cool air conditioning felt amazing after the humidity, giving me a little extra spring to help drag Nic back to my room. Ash hurried down the hallway ahead of us to get the door.

We got Nic in my room, and she shut the door behind us. "What happened?"

"I don't know. You saw Mary in the mirror over the fireplace?"

"No, I missed that moment of reliving childhood terror," she said dryly.

"She's injured," I said, as we got the prince into my bed.

"She might not have made it," Nic gasped. "She was hurt badly helping me, and they were coming after her. I don't"—he coughed—"I don't know how they did it, but they set loose some sort of demon in the mirror realm."

The effort of getting that out exhausted him, and he fell back, eyes shut.

I pulled away from the prince. Once my touch left him, tremors wracked Nic's body.

"Ember, crawl into bed with Prince Nic and wrap yourself around him. He needs you," Geraint said.

I did what Geraint told me, and Nic quieted.

"What do we do?"

"Does he eat?" Ash asked. "I know I've seen him consume food, but does he actually need to eat?"

"I do," Geraint said with a shrug. "But I'm not sure how that translates to a true Nightmare dweller."

"Let me get you something like broth, and I'll bring dinner for the two of you," Ash said.

"Bring a bunch of water, too?" I asked.

"I will. Knight, come help me, please."

Geraint glanced at me, and I nodded, so they left.

I snuggled tighter around the prince, throwing a leg over his hip and resting my head on his shoulder.

Nic's breathing eased further.

"Ember?" he said after a few minutes of silence.

"Yeah?"

"Are you really there?" His voice was thick with exhaustion.

"Yes, Nic. I'm here."

That seemed to settle him, and his breathing deepened.

I lay there until Ash and Geraint returned with food. Then I sat up to eat, staying in contact with Nic.

"Do you think I should take the essence in my clothing and give it to Nic?"

Geraint tilted his head, considering. "Wait until he wakes up and ask him. It might be good to have a reserve. We have the small amount left in your clothing, and in what I wore. That's it, as far as I know."

"Doesn't seem like much." I hunched my shoulders and concentrated on the food.

"No."

Ash leaned against the door, while Geraint sat in his rocking chair.

"So, what's next?" Ash said.

"I guess we wait for Nic to wake up." I handed Geraint my dishes and snuggled back against Nic's side.

"Okay." Ash ran her hand through her short hair. Her inked arms were on full display in her tank top. "I have court for the next few days. I'll have to call you and check in."

"Yeah, that's fine. Of course you have to work."

"Do not go anywhere without telling me first." She pointed her finger sternly at me, then at Geraint.

"We won't, Ash," I assured my cousin.

"Okay. Phone is on, unless I'm in court. Call me if anything changes, or text me. I need to get home."

"Drive careful, Ash."

She came over to the other side of the bed and gave me a quick hug, punched Geraint on the shoulder, and left.

"I'm torn between seeing if we can get him to eat, and letting him rest," Geraint said.

"Rest, I think."

"Okay." Geraint pulled the blanket at the end of the bed up over both of us. "Just stay there. I'll keep an eye out for trouble."

"Thanks."

"Always, Spark."

My knight slipped out. I did my best to stay awake in case Nic needed something, but his quiet breathing lulled me to sleep.

"Ember." Nic's whisper woke me some time later.

"Nic?"

"We're not safe." His voice sounded stronger than it had. "They'll come for us, here, if they can."

"Geraint is keeping watch. What happened?"

He pulled me tightly against his side. "Baz, or whoever that is, seems to be losing control of what shred of sanity he had. I don't know how they did it, but somehow, they captured me using light. I'd rather not discuss the rest." He shuddered. "Suffice it to say, Mary saved my life. And so did you and your knight."

"I hope you don't mind me sharing a bed with you, but you got all twitchy when I tried to leave you alone." I tightened my grip on him, as he had on me.

"I should think it is obvious I don't mind. I'm grateful. Sharing your energy with me is helping me recover more quickly."

"I gave you the last of the essence I held," I admitted. "We still have the bit stored up in the clothing Geraint and I were wearing if you need it."

"Save it for now, we might need it later." Nic trailed his fingers over my back. His shadow had returned and shifted around us, tendrils of shadow stuff swirling around my body. "Ember, I should very much like to kiss you, if you think Geraint won't mind too much."

I thought back to the conversation we'd had not long before. "No, I don't think he will mind."

Nic rolled over on his side to face me, propped up on one elbow, and threaded one of his legs between my calves. He cupped my cheek with his other hand and pressed his lips to mine.

"I've missed you," he breathed onto my lips. "Your absence from my side has always been noticeable, but after having you back, losing you again created a gaping wound in my heart."

I clutched his shirt with one fist, and buried the fingers of my other hand in his hair.

Our lips spoke without words, and our tongues danced to music only we could hear. My heart soared as energy flowed between us, filling an emptiness I hadn't realized was there. Nic didn't have much to spare, but my human energy flowed back into him, helping him heal.

I moaned softly, and he tightened his grip on me, as if he'd never let go.

"I want to claim you." He kissed along my jawline.

"I can't give up Geraint." I gasped for breath, heart racing, heat pooling in my core.

"That's not a no."

His lips possessed mine again before I could reply. I let myself drown in the desperate attention he consumed me with.

I lost track of time while we kissed, the need deep inside me purring contentedly while still demanding more connection.

The squeak of the door opening barely registered. I was familiar with the sound and ignored it, but Nic froze.

I whimpered when he pulled away, before realizing we weren't alone.

"Ahh, sorry," Geraint said, not sounding terribly upset.

"Nothing to apologize for, Knight," Nic replied, releasing me.

I rolled over onto my stomach, clenching the comforter we lay on in my hands, my legs still entangled with Nic's. The need to be filled roared through me, and I groaned into the bed.

"I asked her if I could kiss her, then couldn't bring myself to stop."

"I think we are both being unfair to Ember," Geraint said, putting his hand on the back of my leg.

"How so?" Nic's hand went to my back, stroking gently.

Having the two of them touching me lit a fire that thundered through me. I twisted, rubbed my legs together, clutching the comforter like a lifeline. I was about to kick both of them out and dive between my legs with my hand and the nearest toy. The level of need I felt drove coherency out of the window.

"She wants both of us," Geraint said. "I never expected to get to keep her, but I can't imagine giving her up now. I'm willing to share if you are.

"I realize you're a prince and I'm only a knight, but Ember knew nothing of this when we came together. I love her, and I can't live without her, but none of us can live without Dream or Nightmare."

"I don't know if the others would find that acceptable." Nic curled his fingers in my hair.

"If they want in my pants, they've got to accept Knight," I grumbled. "And I'm pretty sure you want in my pants."

Nic chuckled. "Indeed, I do. Ember, if we come together and complete the bond that we started all those years ago, you will be the Nightmare princess. There's no going back. Deciding that in your current state might not be wise."

"What does being your princess entail?" I forced myself to think of something other than getting someone's cock in my aching pussy.

"Truthfully, the biggest commitment is spending time in Nightmare, enriching the dreamlands with your energy. It doesn't mean you have to stay forever. It doesn't even mean you have to keep sleeping with me."

I snorted at that. "Unless you're terrible in bed, that's not going to be an issue if we do this."

"I hope not," Nic replied. "I've not been with anyone else, so I can't say for sure. Though, I'm familiar with the process. It's a common theme in dreams."

That startled me. I unburied my face from the blankets and turned to look at him.

He had a faint smile on his face.

"Oh. Well. You're a great kisser, so I doubt you'll suck at the rest."

Nic's smile broadened. "I leave it up to you to decide if you want to find out. I agree with Geraint. I can share with him if that's what you want."

I looked at my knight. He nodded encouragement. "I'm fine with it, really, Spark."

"Things in Nightmare are more complicated than normal. I can't say what you'll have to get involved with if you become our princess in truth, not just in name. I had hoped to leave you out of the conflict, but I don't think I can. Robby was right. We are weak right now, and together we are stronger. We have to stop Baz and whatever is going on. The nothingness has gotten worse since you left."

"Where is Robby?" I hadn't even thought of him earlier.

"Looking for the real Baz. We think Dio is in the conscious realm. Baz trapped me while I was attempting to rescue Mary so I could come look for Dio. Instead, she rescued me."

Ignoring the aching need between my legs as best I could, I thought about Mary's terrifying visage, and how nice she truly was, and the sacrifice she'd made to get Nic to safety. I thought about the sex demons, and the crazy landscape, and the wolves, and even the terrifying creatures that had helped me escape fake Baz in the first place. The strange darkness of Nightmare, and the flat colors of the boundary lands. I thought of how much I wanted to see Dream. The creatures in Nightmare had likely given their lives for me, not knowing a thing about me other than that I was their princess. I owed it to them to help put things to rights in Nightmare. The simple path and returning to the life that I'd created would be easier, but I'd played a silly childhood game and inadvertently bound myself to the princes of Nightmare. I could still have the life I wanted, after I helped save a land that had given so much to save me.

Really, in the end, there wasn't a lot left to debate.

"I'll be your Nightmare princess."

CHAPTER 20

Nic

Time stopped when Ember said yes. Though I finally decided I wanted her, I hadn't expected this moment to ever happen. I stared into her beautiful brown eyes, overcome with emotion.

"It's not very late yet," Geraint said. "I'll keep watch. Take your time."

"Geraint." Ember pulled her gaze away from mine and turned to look at her knight. Her brow furrowed with worry.

"Ember, it's okay. This works for everyone. We'll figure out the details later. I'll keep an eye on things."

"Knight," I said, suddenly needing to make sure he understood how immediate the danger was. "It's possible they know Dio is in the conscious realm. They'll be trying to get rid of all of us now, and they've recruited some of the more powerful nightmares to their side. Watch your back."

"I will," he assured us. "And I'll watch yours. Now enjoy yourselves."

He exchanged another long look with Ember before turning away and leaving us alone.

Ember returned her attention to me.

"Are you sure you're up for this?" Ember asked. "You were pretty beat up when we dragged you back here."

"I'm most certainly up for this," I replied with a mischievous smile.

Her eyes widened, and she laughed. "Okay."

"You're sure you want this?" I had to ask one more time.

Instead of answering, her clothes melted away. I hadn't realized she'd been wearing the clothing she'd acquired in Nightmare.

"I'm sure," she replied when I continued to stare. "Do we need to discuss condoms or anything? I'm on birth control and I've only ever been with Geraint."

"The logistics of true procreation are complicated and involve actual intention between a mortal and Dream being, and as I said, I've never been with anyone. We should be safe."

"Okay. Great, because I don't actually have any."

Ember had a magnificently muscular body, honed from years of gymnastics and circus.

Hesitantly, I extended my hand. Some of my shadow followed it, as if it took on a mind of its own and wanted to touch, too.

"Nic, I said yes. It's okay to touch me."

I took a deep breath and nodded.

She murmured happily when my hand settled on her warm skin, the shadow sliding across her hip as I ran my fingers up her ribs to the curve of her breast.

"So, what sorts of things can you do with those shadows of yours?" She lay back to give me better access to her body.

"Nearly whatever I want." I curled a bit of shadow around her ankle.

Her eyes widened. "Really? Show me."

I frowned, then understood where she was going with her request. "I will do my best."

My shadow slid up her arms, wrapping around her wrists and pinning her to the bed.

"Is this okay?" I asked when her pupils dilated.

"Yes," she replied, breathless.

Trailing my fingers along her stomach and teasing her breasts pulled soft moans from Ember's lips. I sent tendrils of shadow to curl around her legs and wrap up her thighs.

She tilted her knees out. "So many possibilities," she murmured, eyes shut as she enjoyed the attention.

"You may gain similar abilities."

"It's like there are two of you," she purred delightedly as I continued to caress her. The shadows sliding up her legs curled between her legs, and I directed them upward, turning so I could see what I was doing, though I could feel her skin as intimately through the shadows as I could with my fingers.

She writhed under my touch, legs wet as her desire seeped from her. The scent of her arousal perfumed the air and furthered my ache to be buried inside her. Patience, though. I wanted her well and truly sated before I took my pleasure.

Ember trembled when the shadows caressed her soaked lips. I curled one tendril inside her like a finger, rubbing her inner walls, while I placed another over her clit and fashioned it much like a sucker and put it to work.

"Oh, my god!" she cried out, arching up off the bed and crying out wordlessly.

"Too much?"

"No, holy crap, that's amazing." Ember's muscles contracted around my shadows, tightening, before letting go and rippling around the shadows I'd twined inside her. The sensation was absolutely exquisite, and I wanted it again.

Gently, I brushed my hands across her soaked pussy. She groaned and pushed against me.

I put the shadow inside her to work, curling along her walls, sliding deeper while she urgently cried out my name.

It didn't take long to have her trembling and on the edge of release again. I eased up, not wanting to bring her over too soon.

"Nic," she gasped. "I'm so close!"

"I know, luv."

She made a delightedly frustrated sound, shoving herself against the shadows I invaded her body with as best as she could, while I still had her restrained.

Chuckling, I gave in and let her have what she wanted.

Ember cried out, and I spared a moment to hope we were alone on this end of the house. Of course, I imagined she and the knight weren't quiet, so they'd probably sorted that problem years ago. I could find out, but I didn't want to take my attention any further from the beautiful woman quivering beneath me.

"Fuck, Nic, you're still wearing clothing."

"Much like yours, I can fix that instantly."

"Strip, Prince. I want your cock buried in me," she ordered.

"My shadows aren't good enough?" I stroked them in and out of her.

"They're plenty good, but I want more."

I laughed and shifted my clothing into the shadows so I was bare. I didn't make myself completely solid, but the important parts were.

She grinned at me, eyes traveling down my body. Her tongue darted out of her mouth, flicking across her lips. "Yeah, let's do this," she said.

My shadows still filled her, and I slid them out, making sure she felt it as they left.

Ember's lips parted in pleasure. "For someone who's never done this before—"

I pressed myself against her entrance. "It's not as if I didn't have access to millions of dreams on the subject."

She laughed and rolled her hips, encouraging me.

"Can I have one of my hands back? I want to touch you."

"Of course." I pulled the tendril of shadow away from her wrist, sliding it down her arm, and cupping her breast with it.

I slid inside her, reveling in the feel of her slick walls trembling around my cock, tight and warm and welcoming and everything I could have ever imagined. Ember wrapped her legs around my waist, and I rocked into her.

"You feel amazing," she said, threading her fingers into my hair and pulling me down to kiss her.

My energy of Nightmare and hers of the conscious realm coiled around each other like cats rubbing together, warm and soft and purring at the contact, eager to be joined. I was ready. Why had I ever resented that we'd been bound as children? I couldn't even remember at this point, so grateful she'd chosen to allow me back into her life.

We moved together, my climax building just as hers was.

I wrapped my shadows around her, holding her close, trying to promise without words that I'd never let her go.

"Nic, this is so amazing. You're amazing. Let's do this all the time. There are so many things I want to try." She let her head fall back, mouth open as she keened with her building release.

"That's a fantastic idea, Ember," I gasped out.

"Oh, I'm coming again." She bucked her hips underneath me.

I let her release take me over the edge into my own.

Our energies joined, my shadows sinking into Ember where they touched her, tying us together and tying her to Nightmare. I nearly collapsed on top of Ember at the intensity of the binding.

She dug her fingers into my shoulder, trembling.

"I feel like you're a part of me," she whispered.

"Technically," I panted. "I am right now." I tried to pull the shadows away, but every part of me was almost too sensitive to move. A pleasant torture as I slowly tried to work my shadows free.

"Oh." She looked up at the arm to see the shadows sunken into her skin. "That's trippy."

I laughed. "You should feel it on my end."

"You can feel that?"

"Yes, it's intensely sensitive right now."

"Bad or good?"

"Very good, Ember." I couldn't help trying to shift inside her, and she groaned, eyes fluttering shut and hips thrusting toward me. I loved how sweat had plastered her hair to her skin, and how her muscles tensed under me, and the feel of my weight on top of her.

I couldn't wait for her to ride me, and to try everything else we could possibly imagine.

Eventually, we untangled ourselves and threaded our legs together. She was so wet, between her juices and my fluids seeping from her body. They coated my leg, too.

"Nic?" she murmured sleepily, after I'd held her for a while.

"Yes, Ember."

"How long before we can go again?"

"Probably not too long. I recover quickly."

"So." She grinned at me. "Good first time?"

"I can't even describe how much better that was than I could possibly have imagined," I admitted.

"When do I get my jizz-induced nightmare powers?"

"Your what? Oh." I laughed. "I don't know."

"Mmm, well, I want them soon, so let's keep going until I can do all these cool things to Geraint, too."

Surprisingly, it didn't bother me when she mentioned the knight and wanting to tie him up with my own abilities.

"Whatever you wish, my princess," I said.

She opened her eyes and met my gaze with her own.

"Whatever?" Her grin turned mischievous.

Hoping I wasn't getting myself into anything too crazy, I nodded. "Anything in my power to grant, Ember."

"Any chance you're okay enough with Geraint to try some, uh, acrobatic sex with us sometime?" She bit her lower lip and sucked it into her mouth.

"I'll think about it," I promised.

"That's not no."

I smiled and kissed her. "No, it's not no."

"Great. Now, tie me up and do naughty things to me until my shadow powers manifest. Or until we have to sleep."

"Only until you get your powers?" I raised an eyebrow.

She giggled. "Remember how I said I wanted to do this all the time?"

"I remember." I coiled my shadows between her legs and caressed her soaked folds.

"Yeah, just like that," she purred.

I pressed my lips to hers, and we kissed while I wrapped my princess up in shadow. Bringing her pleasure was currently my greatest desire. I couldn't fix anything else that was wrong in my world right now, but I could make Ember scream my name and come so many times she begged me to stop.

239

We had an entire host of problems we needed to tackle, the foremost finding Dio before not-Baz's goons did, but right now I just wanted Ember to shatter around me until we were well and truly bound. Nothing would separate us, ever again.

The End
The Nightmare princess's adventures continue in book two, Nightmare's Fall.

About the Author

Dakota has two passions in life: writing and cinnamon tea. Tea so strong she ought to be able to see her future when she drinks it, and the writing? Well, she hopes it makes you see stars when you read it. She creates reverse harem romance novels filled with things that go bump in the night. That handsome werewolf walking down the street? The suave vampire you're just dying to get a taste of? You'll find them enraptured by charming, smart ladies ready to make those bad boys work for their affection. When not writing, Dakota can be found on the back of a horse out on the trail or tending the animals on her farm.

Author's Note

Thank you so much for reading my reverse harem tale! More is coming soon! Reviews are so very important, especially to new authors and are greatly appreciated! Even a line or two will do!

Other Works

Mountain Magic Trilogy (complete)

Becoming
Demon's Touch
Reckoning

Ocean Enchantment Trilogy

Siren's Catch
Siren's Song
Siren's Storm

Pizza Shop Exorcist (complete)

The Price of Possession
The Price of Exorcism
The Price of Magic
The Price of Souls
The Price of Rebellion

Horsemen Against the Apocalypse Duet

Seeking War
Apocalypse Interrupted

Dreambound Trilogy

Nightmare's Dance
Nightmare's Fall
Nightmare's Flight